Compassionate Nails

A Journey of Love and Resilience

(Translated from the Vietnamese title 'Nails Tình Thương')

by

Vinh Q. Tang

ISBN 978-1-7381921-4-4

Nghĩa Lan Nhân

Acknowledgment

The translation of the Vietnamese title "Nails Tình Thương" by the same author has been facilitated with significant assistance from ChatGPT.

Vinh Quyen Tang
Ottawa, 01-01-2024

Contents

1. Twist of Fate

Amidst the static crackle of long-distance calls, a familiar exchange unfolds:

"Hello!"

"Is that you, Mom? It's me here."

"Yes, Mom here."

"How are you, Mom?"

"I'm alright. You two and the two little ones doing well?"

"Yes, Mom, everyone is fine. What time is it over there now?"

"It's nearly 9 in the morning, dear."

"Over here, it's 9 in the evening, Mom."

Thân and his wife have called Canada home for over a decade, yet their hearts remain tethered to Mrs. Sáu, Thân's mother, in Vietnam. Each call, a lifeline across continents, dances with familiar cadences but never loses its warmth.

Their conversations, spanning time zones, often orbit the remarkable achievements of their two children. Through the phone's thin wire, they paint vivid portraits of their offspring's triumphs, each tale a brushstroke of joy for Mrs. Sáu. Whether they sprinkle in a bit of extra zest or embellish the narratives, it matters little, for in these moments, joy transcends distance.

Since Nghĩa, their second child, was born in Canada, the couple's phone bills have swelled - a small price to pay for bridging oceans and sharing milestones.

"Your grandson can turn over now, Mom!"

"Your grandson can crawl now, Mom!"

"Your grandson can stand now, Mom!"

"Your grandson can walk now, Mom!"

And now:

"Your grandson can talk now, Mom."

As Nghĩa embarks on his kindergarten journey, new tales unfold:

"Your grandson is thriving, Mom. Today, he earned a constellation of heart-shaped awards from his teacher!"

Thân and his wife also share their lives with their older daughter, Thảo, born in Vietnam and woven into the fabric of their shared journey, escaping together when she was just six years old.

Upon arriving in Canada, Thảo began attending elementary school, and her academic achievements were frequently shared with her grandmother back in Vietnam. Mrs. Sáu was elated. However, as Thảo grew older, a new concern began to occupy her thoughts.

During their regular calls to check on Mrs. Sáu, she would often remind Thân and his wife, "Your daughter is growing every day, and though I understand you both are busy with work, it's crucial to keep a watchful eye on her."

Two years ago, the Thân family moved into a new, more spacious house, upgrading from their initial home when they started their careers. The new residence boasted numerous rooms, spanning from the upper floors down to the basement, prompting them to wonder, "How do we occupy all of this space?" In response, the couple decided to lease a small room in the basement to a young compatriot acquaintance, not only making the most of their space but also conveniently earning some extra income.

When Mrs. Sáu learned about this, she became very upset. Even just hearing her voice over the phone, Mrs. Thân felt worried, 'I have never seen mom so angry before.' Mrs. Sáu repeatedly reminded Mr. and Mrs. Thân, "Remember you have a daughter in the house," and kept warning them, 'Fire near straw is hard to avoid the stove.' So, the couple had to plead for the 'fire' to be moved elsewhere.

From that point onward, Thân, his wife, and Mrs. Sáu found themselves diligently addressing this high-priority matter, even with the vast ocean separating them. They worked tirelessly to extinguish one 'fire' after another, starting from the moment when the metaphorical 'stoves' were first ignited, even though these stoves only existed in the realm of their imagination.

Yet, as fate would have it, three days ago, when Thảo returned from school, she surprised her parents by announcing her plan to attend a high school prom with a classmate named 'Raul' - a name unfamiliar to Thân and his wife.

Today, Thân urgently called Mrs. Sáu to share some concerning news: "Mom, Thảo has a boyfriend now, and it seems like he's from an Arabic country or somewhere similar," he disclosed. After narrating the entire story, he earnestly requested Mrs.

Sáu's intervention, saying, "Mom, please talk to her. She values your opinion a lot."

"You are closer to her; try to offer your advice. It's challenging for me to say anything from such a distance," Mrs. Sáu responded. Acknowledging their own parenting challenges, Thân admitted, "My wife and I tend to get hot-headed and often end up yelling at her. That would push her away. We plan to call you this weekend so that you can have a talk with her."

"Alright then, let Mom talk to her and see how it goes," Mrs. Sáu agreed.

Thân bid farewell to Mrs. Sáu, feeling a wave of relief wash over him. Everything had been taken care of by 'Mom' just as always. Hanging up the phone, he strolled over to the sofa, savored his tea, and let his gaze wander to the twilight sky beyond the window. As he relaxed, he found himself lost in the echoes of Mrs. Sáu's words, which summoned childhood memories from his hometown.

Forty years ago, beneath the red-tiled roof of a house on the outskirts of Saigon, Thân, then around five years old, would sit on the mosaic floor in the corridor, wide-eyed, observing "Aunt Út" as she performed manicures for Mrs. Sáu every week. Back then, he didn't quite comprehend who Aunt Út was or where she came from; all he knew was that she would occasionally arrive at the house, bearing two baskets. The smaller one contained tools for his mother's nails, while the larger one held a variety of items - Mysteries unveiled only when Aunt Út opened it.

Aunt Út often touted foldable umbrellas and raincoats, but more enticingly, she offered perfumes and cosmetic boxes imported from France and the United States. If that were all, young Thân might not have lingered for hours next to Mrs. Sáu's armchair, watching Aunt Út delicately paint his mother's nails while perched on a small stool.

On occasion, Aunt Út would reveal a children's toy. Mrs. Sáu wasn't particularly fond of them, considering them extravagant, but if she perceived educational value, she wouldn't hesitate to purchase one for her child. It was through this that Thân came to possess a kaleidoscope, a treasure he would cherish for a lifetime. Young Thân found himself captivated by peering through the eyepiece, fixating on the kaleidoscopic patterns at the end of the scope. The experience became even more enchanting as he learned to manipulate the lens with his fingers, each slight rotation revealing a new, vibrant, and mesmerizing pattern.

Decades later, in a foreign land, Thân found himself earning a living in the very profession Aunt Út had practiced back in the day. Not only that, but he and his wife also established roots in the business after taking over a nail salon from an acquaintance. Life unfolded rapidly, akin to the shifting patterns in a kaleidoscope, emerging with each turn and fading just as swiftly. Thân squinted, attempting to envision...

In the sky, a Celestial Offspring peered through a kaleidoscope at Thân's life. At first, he saw a young child eagerly awaiting toys hidden in the nail technician's bag.

Gently shaking the kaleidoscope, the Celestial Offspring glimpsed a small boy in a white shirt riding his bike to school every day.

Shaking it again, he beheld the same boy, now neatly dressed in a green military uniform at an army camp.

Once more, the boy transformed into a man, clad in earth-toned clothes, embracing his wife and child on a refugee boat amid an ocean expanse.

Intrigued, the Celestial Offspring shook it again, revealing a 'Nails' salon owner in a gray trench coat strolling through the snow-white sky.

Though intrigued, the Celestial Offspring couldn't help but wonder about the origins of such a peculiar and coincidental trajectory. It seemed as though the grip of destiny, or shall we say, the claws of 'the hands' in this case, have clung to a person from childhood to adulthood, from the ancestral homeland to a foreign land.

After pondering for a while, the Celestial Offspring suddenly exclaimed, "I understand now."

Mr. Celestial Father, sipping tea nearby, stirred and inquired, "What have you learned?"

The young Celestial Offspring eagerly responded, "I have discovered why, in the earthly realm, during a Thúy Nga's show, singer Trang Thanh Lan remarked, 'Even shoes have their own Numbers.'"

Celestial Father explained, "People refer to that as 'fate' or 'destiny,' predetermined by the heavens."

Curious, the Celestial Offspring asked, "Father, I've assisted you in managing all the records for Heaven, but I have never come across the book of 'Numbers' anywhere?"

Celestial Father admonished, "Do you mean Lottery? As a celestial being, be cautious not to engage in gambling and risk losing your wings, my child."

The Celestial Offspring clarified, "No, Father. I am referring to the heavenly book that documents each person's 'Number.'"

"Well, there is no such book of destiny in the heavens, but exercise discretion and refrain from discussing it. If people were aware of it, everyone would attempt to dictate their own 'Number,' leading to inevitable chaos in the world."

At this juncture, Thân suddenly smiled, content with his fate and his present circumstances. He strode purposefully to the computer room, preparing to calculate the wages for the nail technicians due tomorrow.

2. A Daughter in the House

As dawn breaks, a rosy hue envelops the 'Golden Boy' statue, its gleaming form reaching skyward like an angel overseeing Manitoba's legislative building in Canada. The moniker 'Golden Boy' suits this gold-plated statue, embodying the spirit of the Roman god Mercury, thoughtfully chosen by legislators to symbolize youthfulness and entrepreneurial vigor. Capturing the essence of this representation is a muscular youth, torch aloft, legs poised in a running stance, and gaze directed northward, embracing the vast and resource-rich northern region of the province.

Behind the wheel of a cream-colored station wagon, Thân chauffeurs his wife to the heart of Winnipeg to open their nail salon. This particular vehicle, broader and longer than the standard household sedan, is a favored choice among North American middle-class families for weekend getaways and extended journeys. Its spacious interior ensures the entire family can sit comfortably, with ample room in the rear for luggage - a dual-purpose solution appreciated by the Thâns. It efficiently accommodates the transportation of bulk goods for the nail salon while also serving as a family travel companion for holiday escapes or summer adventures.

As the car approaches the inner city, Thân eagerly anticipates the brief stretch of road leading to the park in front of the legislative building, offering him the chance to admire the brilliant radiance of the 'Golden Boy.' Even in those fleeting moments on the roadside, lasting only a couple of minutes while waiting for the traffic light, it is enough to evoke a delightful and exhilarating feeling in Thân before embarking on the familiar routine of daily activities. Seated beside him, Mrs.

Thân absentmindedly contemplates their own "golden boy," their youngest son, whom they had just left at Mrs. Tư's home daycare.

"Hey, I think we should buy a small TV for the office so that our child can watch it every afternoon after school," Mrs. Thân suggests.

The place referred to as the 'office' by Mrs. Thân is a small room nestled behind the nail salon. It features a work desk, two cushioned chairs acquired from a military surplus store, and three small stools for the nail technicians to use during lunchtime.

This year, their son Nghĩa has reached the age to start first grade, with school scheduled to begin next month. Mr. and Mrs. Thân's plan is to pick Nghĩa up from school every day and bring him to the salon, where he can play in the office with a few nail technicians watching over him, thus avoiding the expense of sending him to an external daycare.

A few days ago, Mrs. Thân brought two boxes of toys from home to keep in the room, but she still worries about whether their child needs anything else.

After hearing his wife's suggestion to buy a TV, Thân glances at her with a half-eye and says, "Buy a TV for the kid, or for his mom?" Mrs. Thân bashfully admits, "Well, if I have some free time, I can watch some old music video tapes rather than letting them gather dust at home."

The video tapes "gather dust" not because the couple doesn't enjoy music; quite the contrary, they are so passionate about Vietnamese music that they keep buying a lot and end up being unable to finish listening to all of them. The tapes are stored in seven cardboard boxes in the basement of their home. Whenever the family travels to cities with a significant Vietnamese community, there are three places they must visit without fail: Vietnamese restaurants, Vietnamese markets, and Vietnamese music video tape stores. The pirated video tapes are sold at a much lower price, less than half the cost of an original tape, so the couple often buys dozens of them to bring home and watch.

Thân suddenly remembers something and says, "You shouldn't watch those tapes; someday the authorities might catch you."

Mrs. Thân looks at her husband askance in reproach, "Why would they catch me?"

"Well, because you're watching pirated tapes."

"Come on, everyone watches them; it's not a big deal."

Thân chuckles, "Don't you see that now the video tapes have FBI warnings on them?"

"In Canada, we don't have the FBI[1] to be afraid of."

"But we have the RCMP[2]."

Thân reflected on how, in recent times, show producers had frequently appeared in their videos, expressing concerns about the widespread piracy of their music albums. They earnestly implored viewers to support them by purchasing the original products from their companies. As a businessman, Thân couldn't help but empathize with the challenges faced by these video entertainment companies. Filled with a sense of responsibility, he confided in his wife, "It's because of people seeking bargains, much like yourself, that the pirated tapes industry thrives."

Mrs. Thân grunted in response, "Sounding as if you dislike bargains. Placing blame on others!"

In an attempt to downplay the issue, Thân replied, "Actually, many people listen to pirated CDs, not just us."

However, Mrs. Thân, maintaining a poised demeanor, countered, "Don't you recall what our daughter said? They teach her in school,

---

[1] FBI: Federal Bureau of Investigation.
[2] RCMP: Royal Canadian Mounted Police

'What's wrong is wrong; it can't become right just because many people do it.'"

After a moment of silence, Thân burst into laughter. Intrigued, Mrs. Thân asked, "Why are you laughing?"

"Just remembering what our daughter Thảo said. When she was only 9 years old, she caught me trying to copy a music tape, and she blurted out a sentence that stunned us both, 'I thought our house was the most legal house in the world.'"

Mrs. Thân chuckled, "We were completely speechless after hearing that." Seizing the moment to share her thoughts, she continued, "It's all because of you, and no one else. You're as cautious as a rabbit, afraid of breaking any laws. While others receive substantial tax returns every year, you not only declare everything honestly but also harbor the fear that the government would suspect you of cheating. It's admirable, but I can't help but wonder if your excessive fear is holding you back."

"I truly admire your talent. Here we are, praising our daughter, and you manage to bring up the topic of tax filing."

"Well, it's because you're cautious about everything, and you inadvertently teach the kids to be the same way."

Thân smiled awkwardly. He didn't intend to blame his wife or anyone else for any wrongdoing. He just instinctively sought solace for his soul to feel more comfortable continuing to watch overseas Vietnamese musical programs, driven by the urge to see familiar faces, hear familiar voices, and revive the joys and sorrows of a past that now seems like it belongs to a previous life.

When Thảo was mentioned, a shared concern weighed heavily on the hearts of Mr. and Mrs. Thân. Mrs. Thân remarked, "Mom was right. Having 'a daughter in the house' is like having a timed bomb." She sighed, "If only we had known back then, we would have let her attend Vietnamese language classes to make Vietnamese friends."

Thân pondered, "At that time, there weren't Vietnamese language schools like there are now."

Mrs. Thân reminded her husband: "There were. Teacher Hồng opened a class at her home. You forgot?"

"Oh, now I remember. I thought by the time we moved here, our child was already grown, and she spoke Vietnamese fluently, so we decided to let her have more time to focus on learning English to keep up with schoolwork."

Mrs. Thân added, "I also remember: one of the reasons was that the school was already teaching both English and French. We thought if we forced her to learn Vietnamese as well, she might have to struggle and end up not proficient in any language."

Thân sighed, blaming himself for how their daughter had turned out. "It's hard to anticipate everything in life. Just hope that mom won't think that we have neglected the kids."

Mrs. Thân chimed in, "Well, you are always afraid that we might be too strict with the kids, making it more difficult for them to live independently later on in their lives."

Mr. Thân pondered, "Here, people come from all corners of the world. Seeing how smart and audacious other kids are, when looking at our own child, she seems so naive. I wonder if she'll be able to compete when she enters the rat race."

The two spouses fell into a silent contemplation, grappling with concerns about the future of their children in a foreign land.

3. A Lesson in Geography

In the evening, after a satisfying dinner, the Thân family gathered closely in the entertainment room. Three sofas of varying lengths, generously cushioned and arranged in a semi-circle, hosted the family members in front of the latest and largest television money could buy. Mr. and Mrs. Thân made a conscious effort to engage with their children, tuning into a TV game show titled 'Family Dispute' to keep everyone entertained. Despite the language barrier and imperfect auditory skills, the Thâns were content as long as watching TV brought joy to their children.

Typically, they had to wait for about half an hour, allowing the older child to depart for her studies and the younger one to head to bed, before relishing some private space to indulge in the drama series from Hong Kong or Korea. However, on a day when a new Vietnamese music video was available at the store, it felt as if the tape had magically appeared in their own home as well. Naturally, it took precedence for screening on the wide TV screen, eagerly anticipated by the family, akin to people awaiting rain in a drought or children eagerly awaiting candy.

Mrs. Thân stared intently at the TV, engrossed in the 'Family Dispute' show, yet puzzled and unable to comprehend what the program host was saying. "What did he ask, dear?" she inquired.

Thảo, always quick to assist her mother, replied, "He asked: According to a survey of 100 women, what is the most obvious sign for a wife to know that her husband is having an affair?"

Upon hearing this, Mrs. Thân didn't directly respond to her daughter but shot her husband a sharp, dagger-like look, saying, "You better watch out."

Mr. Thân quickly responded, "What do you mean?"

"Acting like I don't know, but these past few days, I've seen you buzzing around the girl from the New Market a lot," Mrs. Thân accused.

"Well, I noticed that she was from our hometown, so I wanted to ask if she knew anyone from our former neighborhood," Mr. Thân explained. Mrs. Thân grumbled, "What kind of girl dresses like a queen for work?" She then threw a warning look in her husband's direction and provided her own answer, "To catch some 'naive fish' like you." Mr. Thân shook his head, "Well, wasn't that your idea, asking the workers to tidy up and look presentable to attract customers?"

The intriguing narrative of the husband and wife hinted at a promising sequel. However, as Mrs. Thân listened to her husband, she remained silent, directing her gaze to the slender Seiko gold-plated clock firmly affixed to the eggshell-colored wall behind the family dining table. Without uttering a word, she stood up and summoned her youngest child. "It's almost eight-thirty. Win, go upstairs and sleep."

Win, or Nghĩa, and Nghĩa, or Win - his name carried a unique tale. Born in Winnipeg, the grandmother from Vietnam had sent the name Nghĩa for the parents to bestow upon him. As Nghĩa grew up and ventured into daycare, no one, from friends to daycare staff, managed to pronounce the Vietnamese name correctly. Therefore, Mr. and Mrs. Thân assigned to him an English name, Win, expressing gratitude to Winnipeg - the city that had provided refuge to their family during the initial days of seeking sanctuary. Beneath it all, they harbored a hope that the English name would bring good fortune, symbolizing 'winning' success in their endeavors. Yet, most importantly, the English name was chosen for its simplicity of pronunciation, a convenience not lost on Mr. and Mrs. Thân.

With a hint of reluctance, Win rose to follow his mother, earning Mrs. Thân's praise for his obedience. After a couple of steps, she turned back to address Thảo. "Thảo, go to your room and study." "I still have a whole week off to review, Mom," Thảo replied, thinking she had escaped. Quickly she realized it was futile with Mrs. Thân. Continuing on her way, Mrs. Thân offered a piece of advice. "Study a little every day so that it sinks in, instead of waiting until the last minute and cramming without understanding anything."

Thân sat, observing Thảo intently. "Are you still planning to attend the school party with that 'Rệp' guy?" he inquired. Thảo raised her eyebrows in response. "Dad! He is not 'Rệp'." "Well, but he's an Arab, right?" Thân questioned. Thảo shook her head. "I told you, Dad, he's Lebanese."

Mrs. Thân descended the stairs, plopped onto the sofa beside Thân, and reluctantly joined the conversation. "Well, he's still from Africa, right? Mom and Dad have told you that you should choose someone Vietnamese. That would be more suitable. Otherwise, a person from Asia is also fine."

Thảo responded with enthusiasm, "That's good then." Mrs. Thân looked puzzled, exchanging a skeptical glance with her husband.

Thảo explained, "Raul is also from Asia because Lebanon is in Asia. Our Vietnam is in the eastern part of the Asian continent, while Lebanon is in the west." Mr. Thân persisted in his argument, "But he speaks Arabic, so he must be an Arab." Thảo calmly corrected him, "He doesn't speak Arabic. His family speaks French." Mrs. Thân was surprised, and Mr. Thân wondered, "So, what ethnicity is he?" "I told you guys before; he is Lebanese," Thảo reiterated. Thân tried to dismiss it, "So, he's a Muslim, right? Muslims are often violent." Thảo shook her head in dismay. "Dad, that's prejudice. No religion is inherently violent. At school, I have many Muslim friends. All of them are very gentle and lovely."

Thân resisted, "I know there are good and bad people everywhere, but how can we, outsiders, distinguish which one is kind and which one is aggressive? Or which one is just an ordinary person and which one is a 'bomb holder'?" Thân was referring to extremist elements, those who engage in armed conflicts and are not afraid to carry bombs into enemy territory. Thảo corrected him, "Raul follows the Christian faith, Dad." Mr. and Mrs. Thân's prejudices had just been shattered. Reality was far from their preconceptions. Nevertheless, Mr. Thân still clung to the stereotypical image of a Lebanese person in his imagination. He shook his head in frustration, saying, "In any case, they still look different. It's difficult, my child."

Thảo was genuinely angry with her father. "Dad! How could you say such discriminatory things? Even though Raul has a Caucasian look, there's no need to know what a person's color is. Haven't you heard that the skin color is only as deep as the outer layer of the skin? It doesn't reveal anything about a person, whether they are good or bad, malicious or kind." Thân bowed his head in remorse. He was not unfamiliar with lectures on social etiquette in Canada that his child had brought home from school to 'educate' her parents.

Suddenly, Thân gazed outside, a smile playing on his lips as an intriguing thought crossed his mind. Memories flooded in - of the numerous times Thảo had the opportunity to converse with her grandmother in Vietnam over the phone. The elder never missed a chance to instill in her the importance of good manners, especially in adhering to 'our people's traditions.' In the vast expanse of the cosmos, where planets tugged and pulled at each other, a child in a distant land yearned for her parents to embrace the lifestyle of the new world. Simultaneously, grandparents in the homeland gently reminded their grandchildren residing on foreign soil to uphold the cherished values of 'our people.'

Thân gazed affectionately at his child and began to explain, "Our way of speaking is just like that, my child. Depending on someone's skin color, we might use terms like white, black, or even identify ourselves as yellow people. It's important to note that these descriptors carry no discriminatory intent. However, when it comes to the marriage of our children, there is often a preference for individuals from the same homeland. This tradition may trace its origins back to a time when lives were confined within the bamboo hedges of a typical Vietnamese village."

Taking a thoughtful sip of tea, he continued, "Nevertheless, I recognize that things are different here. This is a land of immigrants, and for the sake of a harmonious and stable society, interracial marriage should not only be accepted but encouraged." Before completing his sentence, Thân felt compelled to add a disclaimer, "Although, in reality, such marriages are still relatively uncommon." Thảo retorted, "Oh my

God, Dad, what are you saying? Who said anything about getting married? Maybe I'll just hang out with Raul this time, and we'll never meet again."

Mr. and Mrs. Thân simultaneously asked, "What are you saying?"

"Come September, when we go to college, he might go to a school in the West, while I'll be heading to the East. How can we meet then?"

Mrs. Thân was surprised. "I thought you were dating him." "Mom! I've never hung out with him before. Date, when?" Mrs. Thân couldn't hide her happy smile, asking Thảo, "Then why do you plan to go to the prom with him?" "The teacher felt sorry for a couple of 'lonely' ones like us, so she arranged a drawing to pair us up and go to the party together for fun," Thảo explained.

Thân sighed in relief, looking at his wife with a half-smile, "Seriously, you are really good at jumping to conclusions! Unfairly accusing my child." Mrs. Thân nudged her husband, "Yeah, wonder who could not eat nor sleep in the last few days, and actually almost phoned home to Vietnam to talk to mom again, huh?" Thân chuckled, admitting that he had secretly called and discussed Thảo's matters with his mother. He looked at Thảo with a playful smile, "Before going to the party, remember to visit the salon and ask the aunties for a manicure. The daughter of the salon owner must have the most beautiful nails in town, OK!"

4. Echo from the homeland

After dinner, Mrs. Thân efficiently tidied up the kitchen. Once satisfied that the leftover food had adequately cooled, she transferred it to a container, sealed it, and placed it neatly in the refrigerator. Moving to the family room, she settled in front of the TV, her mind wandering to the whereabouts of her husband. To her surprise, he emerged from the basement of the house. She raised an eyebrow at Mr. Thân, "Did you just call Mom?" "How do you manage to sit there and know everything?" he replied. "Well, I have three heads, six hands, and twelve eyes to oversee this household, you know."

Thân, silently acknowledging his guilt, approached the DVD player, sat down on the carpet, and held up two music tapes from the TV stand, asking, "Asia or Thúy Nga? We got two new video tapes today. Who wants to watch which one first?" "I want to watch both," Thảo replied promptly. Mrs. Thân nudged her daughter, "If only she had the same enthusiasm for studying." Regretting her harsh words, Mrs. Thân reached over to tuck a strand of hair behind her daughter's ear, trying to glimpse the image of herself over twenty years ago - a diligent student with a good reputation at school. As for Thảo, in the recent academic year, she had achieved high scores in various subjects, giving her parents cause to proudly share the news with her grandmother in Vietnam every time they spoke with her.

The eagerly anticipated moment had arrived, and the "Show" was about to begin. However, Mrs. Thân couldn't shake her curiosity and felt compelled to ask her husband, "What did you say to mom?" "Oh, just asking about her health, nothing special." "But, I talked to her just the other day." After saying that, Mrs. Thân suddenly burst into laughter, "Okay, I know now." Discreetly pointing a finger towards

Thảo, Mrs. Thân whispered, "Let mom know that it's all resolved, so she doesn't worry anymore?" Thân smiled shyly as he was exposed.

Mrs. Thân sat next to him, fixing her gaze on the TV screen as if two laser beams were burning away all the distractions that had followed her throughout the day - from worrying about her husband and children to planning meals not only for today but also for tomorrow and perhaps even the upcoming week. Amidst these concerns, there were, of course, numerous other matters that required her attention at the nail salon.

Thảo sat alone, crossing her legs on a small cushioned chair beside her parents' sofa. Her smile, its origin unknown, adorned her face as her head swayed to the beat of the lively opening music. In the family's midst, a single bright screen captivated their attention. The melodic tunes filling the dreamy space of the cozy room opened countless doors to the soul, leading down myriad paths of the past. Poetic lyrics and musical notes sowed clouds, making rain fall in the heart and storms drop in the soul, arousing waves of tender longing and nostalgic memory. The enchanting music lulled Mrs. Thân into the dreams of her youth and brought her husband back to the aspirations of his past. It also guided the youth through bewildering steps to the legendary homeland of their parents.

The melodies, with no discernible beginning or end, flowed like streams around the hills of Vietnam and meandered beside ripe rice fields. They echoed the folk chants and familiar songs resonating across the three regions of the country, extending along the historical timeline from one generation to the next. Like a magical spell, the sound waves originating from the depths of the soul had the ability to narrow spatial distances, blur the marks of time, and intertwine memories of Hanoi with the pain of Saigon in people's hearts. "*I left Hanoi at the age of eighteen when I first fell in love. So many beautiful dreams of love turned into smoke and vanished with the evening clouds...*" The longing for Hanoi, twenty years ago, had not diminished when the sorrow of parting from Saigon, twenty years later, arrived. "*Saigon, oh, I've lost you in my life. Saigon, oh, the wonderful time has come to an end...*"

Mr. and Mrs. Thân sat in front of the TV, immobile, seeking refuge from life's storms, eagerly awaiting what lay ahead. Their anticipation was not just for a new singer or a good song but also for an unfamiliar "skit," a hilarious comedy - a gateway to remember, to cherish, to cry, and to laugh through the passing days and months. They were waiting to embrace the new in order to rediscover the old. Enthusiastically, they greeted today's artists who were the stars of yesterday, yearning for the resounding voices of the past. Their quest led them to the lyrics and music that carried the sweetness of mother's milk, the tranquil lullaby of the homeland, and the familiarity of the first cradle. In their search, they sought a harbor for the boat swaying in the unpredictable river of life.

However, for Mrs. Thân, no matter how irresistible the allure of the stage lights was, and even if the folk songs sung could transport her back to Chợ Mới, Long Xuyên, where she had cried her first cry and woven her initial dreams, she never strayed too far from reality. It was right on the wall, beside her eyes, ...tick...tick...tick, counting the time next to her ear. She glanced at the clock hanging on the wall, then turned to remind her daughter, "Thảo, it's time to go to bed, my dear." Thảo turned gently, hugging the soft square pillow tightly to her chest as if fortifying herself to fully enjoy the lively and dynamic dance of the graceful dancers.

Mrs. Thân suddenly glanced at her husband and asked, "Have you seen the nail designs of those young singers? People in Cali (California) use those nowadays." Mr. Thân exclaimed, "Seriously, no shoptalk here. Are we watching the show or the nails?" Mrs. Thân nudged her husband, "And what about you? What do you watch, thinking I don't know?" "Well, I am watching fashion." "See, you admitted it." Mrs. Thân shook her head in exasperation, "Our singers in the past didn't dress to shock. They simply wore our traditional 'áo dài' (the long tunic), but looked so elegant and sophisticated." Mr.

Thân attempted to explain, "Art is exploration, my dear. Artists always seek something new to serve the audience. Especially in the overseas context, particularly for the generations that grew up here, they also undergo a journey of self-discovery."

"Actually, there are many new singers I want to watch, but I still admire the ones from the past. How did those ladies maintain their elegance for so long?" "Well, those ladies truly fit the saying, 'Blessed with both beauty and talent.' Like the artist Út Bạch Lan in the Vietnamese reformed opera. Look at her; she seems genuinely kind, exuding a very dignified and graceful style." "Yeah, I heard her life was very tough when she was young. She was homeless and had to sleep in the market at night." "That's why you see, wealth, poverty, or profession doesn't define a person's character. In the past, these artists were even looked down upon with prejudices. Looking back now at the advancements in our contemporary and traditional music, we realize their significant contributions."

Thân took a sip of tea, "Beyond the artistic aspect, I think their style in front of the audience also contributes to creating the beautiful images of a cultured Vietnamese lady." Mrs. Thân nodded in agreement, "Absolutely, every one of them looks affable and virtuous. They often carry themselves with the solemnity of a respectable lady." After a moment, she continued with a smile, "Besides, I admire those ladies for another reason. I don't know how they manage to maintain such a slim figure." Thân chuckled, "Aren't the young female singers just as slim? And even more fiery?" Mrs. Thân turned, jokingly scolding her husband, "Haven't you listened to our charming MC? She warned men like you to watch out for 'imitation' stuff on stage nowadays."

That's life; if artists on stage have various ways to express themselves, the audience also has many ways to perceive them. A pretty face with innocent, doe-like eyes, or a pair of gracefully curved lips, or a coyly hidden smile may bring a sky of romantic greenery and a dreamy golden sunshine for Mr. Thân. On the other hand, for Mrs. Thân, that same face might offer a lesson in applying powder, lipstick, or drawing eyebrows. Perhaps even more curious, she might scrutinize which lips are enhanced, which cheeks are contoured, or which nose has been adjusted, creating an intriguing topic for discussion with her friends at the salon the next day. Pity for the artists, having to face a hundred scrutinizing eyes from their fans.

Thảo was loath to part with the warm, comfortable sofa, reluctantly putting one foot down on the floor. Before she headed upstairs, Mrs. Thân reminded her, "Remember to turn off the soup pot in the kitchen before going up, dear." Seeing Thảo's sleepy eyes that could hardly open, Mrs. Thân felt sorry for her daughter and tried to explain, "Mom is simmering bone broth to make 'Phở' soup for you and your dad." Knowing that 'Phở' is the best-selling dish in the house, she often made it "for Thảo and her dad," even though she herself is allergic to beef.

Looking at Thảo's back, Mrs. Thân nodded knowingly, "The kids here grow up so fast." She reflected quietly before saying to her daughter, "Tomorrow, Mom will buy new pajamas for you." The vague worry about Thảo's 'Arab boyfriend,' which Mrs. Thân thought had been relieved, seems to be just the beginning of other concerns. With Thảo gone, the couple turned off the overseas music program, saving the rest for tomorrow to watch with the children. Mr. Thân leaned down to the video player, inserting a new cassette of 'cải lương' (Vietnamese reformed opera). The couple eagerly began a new journey back to the old place - at a corner of the street, outside an alley, dotted across the city, where day and night echo the familiar classical tunes embraced by the dwellers in these neighborhoods.

5. The palm-leaf hat

Mrs. Thân's primary responsibility revolves around managing the nail salon. Each morning at 8:30, she and her husband arrive at their establishment, 'Bamboo Shoot Nails,' entering discreetly through the back door.

Upon arrival, Mr. Thân heads directly to the office to fulfill Mrs. Thân's directive from the previous day - placing an order for a new batch of nail polish. Once his duties at the salon are complete, he departs for his secondary profession, fixing water pipes for customers, which used to be his primary occupation before venturing into the nail business.

Meanwhile, Mrs. Thân begins her day by traversing from the back to the front of the salon. She systematically switches on the lights, followed by the fan, and then the air conditioner. Although this routine is habitual, regulating the salon's temperature consistently poses a challenge, often causing her headaches throughout the year.

During the summer, maintaining a low temperature for customer comfort leads to increased electricity costs for operating the air conditioner. Conversely, in the winter, ensuring a warm salon environment results in higher heating expenses. While managing these costs is a priority for Mrs. Thân, the human element introduces additional complexities.

In the summer, accommodating Canadian customers with a cool salon prompts complaints from Vietnamese technicians about the cold, impeding their work. Conversely, in the winter, adjusting the temperature to suit Vietnamese technicians results in complaints from Canadian customers about the warmth. Running a business is undoubtedly a challenging task, compounded by these intricacies.

Mrs. Thân swept her gaze across the salon, meticulously observing each nail chair aligned against the left wall and every nail table neatly arranged on the right. Satisfied that all four chairs and five tables were clean, tidy, and ready to welcome customers, she made her way to the front door. There, she spotted Mrs. Năm, a seasoned nail technician at the salon, adorned in her customary conical palm-leaf hat, standing outside the glass door.

The sight of the conical hat evoked a sense of familiarity among the Vietnamese people. However, as Mrs. Thân recalled the first time she saw Mrs. Năm wearing the hat in the snow, she couldn't help but feel perplexed. Where was she, she wondered? If the sun overhead belonged to Saigon, why was it so cold and distant? And amidst the snowy landscape, indicating winter in a foreign land, why did she suddenly feel the warmth of her homeland in her heart? Since her early days living abroad, every winter season, with the streets blanketed in snow, Mrs. Năm always kept the conical hat atop her head, even if she had to wear it over a thick wool toque.

The conical hat had become intertwined with Mrs. Năm's life, an inseparable part of her existence since the day of 'a life-changing event' in her homeland - the South, which had succumbed to defeat in the war against the North. Her husband, a military officer in the South, was taken away for 'reeducation,' and she lost her job as a secretary at a business forced to close by the new regime. In those challenging times, Mrs. Năm not only raised her 9-year-old son but also cared for her frail elderly mother-in-law. She fretted over scraping together every penny to purchase medicine and nutritious food, hoping to provide the best possible support for her ailing husband. However, just a few months later, she received the devastating news of her husband's serious illness and subsequent passing.

The pain of losing her husband compounded the struggle of earning a living to support her family. As economic conditions deteriorated, it eventually pushed Mrs. Năm to sit by the roadside, washing dishes for a stall selling burnt rice marinated with fish sauce near her home every day. By day's end, she would receive a few leftover grains of rice to bring home to feed her family. Throughout the day, she would sit huddled in her conical hat, avoiding the gaze of acquaintances.

A few months later, fate connected Mrs. Năm with a distant relative in Trà Vinh, leading her to join a network that facilitated a daring escape from the country. Advised by her mother-in-law, she saw an opportunity to bring her son, the only grandchild in the family, abroad for education. Once again, the conical hat proved invaluable, helping her conceal her identity from the watchful eyes of the authorities. In their final journey, she and her son took a boat to the open sea, using the conical hat as makeshift shelter to shield themselves from the sun and rain during the uncertain days on the ocean.

Upon settling in Winnipeg, someone unintentionally asked, 'Why don't you take off that conical hat?' Mrs. Năm replied succinctly, 'Used to it.' It remained unclear whether she meant she was accustomed to wearing the conical hat or accustomed to hiding, finding refuge under its shadow.

One winter, she and her son joined a friend on a car trip, traversing over two thousand kilometers on the sometimes icy road to reach Montréal, a large city with a significant Vietnamese community in Canada. Their aim was to celebrate Tết, the Lunar New Year, with fellow compatriots. In Montréal, she felt as if she had struck gold when she saw several conical hats displayed for sale at a booth.

She attempted to purchase the entire inventory of conical hats, but the booth owner declined, regarding them as 'cultural gifts' he wished to share with the community attending the Tết festival, particularly the local residents. Mrs. Năm had to compromise and only bought two, persisting in wearing the conical hat to work to this day.

Mrs. Thân had just opened the door when Mrs. Năm hurriedly stepped into the salon. Suddenly, Mrs. Năm turned her head to look at Mrs. Thân intently, as if she had something to say. Mrs. Thân inquired, "What's the matter, Mrs. Năm?"

Mrs. Năm lowered her conical hat, shaking her head as if trying to dismiss a lingering thought, "Nothing."

Mrs. Thân smiled, recalling her husband's words, 'When someone says there's nothing, there is... something.' She attempted to encourage Mrs. Năm to open up and share her feelings, hoping to address any concerns together and prevent unresolved issues from building up. Mrs. Thân probed further with a more direct question,

"How do you feel about our salon now?"

Mrs. Năm hesitated, "Well, it's okay."

Mrs. Thân pressed on, "How do you feel about our new technician?" The question struck a sensitive chord for Mrs. Năm, "Since you asked, let me tell you." Mrs. Thân reproached gently, "How long have we known each other? You don't have to keep a distance with me like that."

Placing her conical hat in a corner of the reception area, Mrs. Năm stepped out, remarking, "You know, that Hường, she is only as old as my child. I don't have any issues with her. If she's doing well, I'm really happy for her."

In Mrs. Thân's mind, her husband's warning echoed, 'If someone says there's no issue, there is an issue.' Mrs. Thân raised an eyebrow, feigning surprise, "Oh, what did she do?" Although she asked nonchalantly, in her heart, Mrs. Thân thought she already knew the answer. After three years as a technician and several years as the salon owner, Mrs. Thân never once let her guard down; what's going on in the salon couldn't escape her notice.

Mrs. Năm sighed, shook her head, and said, "The little one seems innocent, but she's snatching clients left and right. When I sit next to her, I see it all. As soon as a high-tip client walks in, she seizes them right away. On the other hand, when she encounters a group of potentially low-tip clients, she leaves them for me."

Indeed, Mrs. Thân had already observed this issue with Hường, but she hadn't found a solution yet. The "high-tip" clients Mrs. Năm referred to were those who generously tipped or provided additional bonuses to the technicians, beyond the salon's standard pricing. On the other hand, "low-tip" or "no-tip" clients were those who tipped minimally or not at all.

In the past, the nail technicians in the salon had freely categorized customers based on their skin color, using what could be considered discriminatory language. White customers were described in a certain way, while those with colored skin were portrayed differently. Fortunately, every time little Thảo had a chance to interact with her 'aunties,' as she addresses the technicians, she often advised them against using such language and reminded them that it is not only impolite to customers but also could pose legal issues. The aunts and uncles heeded her advice. From then on, in the salon, they only referred to two types of customers: 'Tê Tê' and 'Tê Q.' 'Tê Tê' represented the 'Tip To' (or big tipper) type, while 'Tê Q' was the type that only said 'Thank You' and left.

Every time a 'Tê Tê' customer entered the salon, regardless of Hường's workload, she would signal to the salon owner, "Let me take care of this." She would then efficiently attend to the current customer to accommodate the new arrival.

However, when a 'Tê Q' customer entered, Hường would employ delaying tactics, appearing deeply engrossed in conversation with the current client and ignoring the newcomer. This behavior understandably irked Mrs. Năm, who spent her days dealing with 'Tê Q' customers and found it frustrating.

Hường's tactics didn't escape the notice of the salon owner. Despite Mrs. Năm's years of experience and reputation as a revered "master instructor" among young technicians, she couldn't match Hường's agility. Furthermore, a language barrier limited Mrs. Năm's communication with customers.

To comfort Mrs. Năm, Mrs. Thân gently patted her shoulder and said, "It's alright, sister. Let me have a word with her. The girl seems open to listening." Mrs. Năm hesitated briefly before consenting, cautioning, "Go ahead and talk to her, but let's not mention the source of the advice to prevent any resentment." Although Mrs. Thân wasn't sure what she would say to Hường, she empathized with Mrs. Năm's dilemma.

In the salon, Mrs. Năm was highly respected and considered a leader within the community. People often turned to her for guidance and support during difficult times, both within the 'family' and beyond the salon walls. Mrs. Năm strived to meet everyone's expectations, often remarking, "Being a good person is hard; being a dog is easy."

In the evening, as Thân drove Mrs. Thân home, she recounted the story of Hường to her husband, seeking his opinion, "This is a delicate matter, I'm not sure how to handle it. Hường is new, but she's highly skilled. She has the expertise and can speak English well. Customers love to chat with her; she often makes them laugh."

Thân furrowed his brows, contemplating, "You're afraid that bringing it up might offend her, and she might leave for another salon, right?" "Yes," Mrs. Thân replied, "Hường's really good. She can leave us and work anywhere. But if we don't say anything, it's unfair to Mrs. Năm. She is like family to us."

"If Hường's that good, let's give her an additional bonus to prevent her from competing with others," Thân suggested.

"Right, but what kind of bonus do you have in mind?" Mrs. Thân asked.

After giving it some thought, Thân said, "Right now we split the earnings sixty-forty with her, right?" At Thân's nail salon, there was an agreement between the owner and the technicians - The technicians get 60 percent of the money earned from each customer, while the remaining 40 percent belongs to the salon owner.

Thân then advised his wife, "Now, you can propose to give Hường an extra one or two percent. It's up to you to decide the exact number." Mrs. Thân sighed, "I'm afraid it won't work. If other technicians find out, they'll turn against us."

"If you tell Hường not to say anything, no one would know."

"Well, I don't like secrecy, doing things discreetly like that. Everything should be open and straightforward. Besides, if Mrs. Năm finds out about this, we might lose all trust. We need to be honest and transparent."

"Then, I would suggest adding a new clause to our policy. In addition to the 60 percent, the technicians can also receive an extra 1 to 5 percent as a bonus, depending on their experience."

"Talking about experience, Mrs. Năm has the most experience. So how is it fair to give a bonus to Hường but not Mrs. Năm?"

Thân didn't miss the opportunity, smiling and saying, "Oh, that's true. It's really difficult; I don't know how to make it right. Or maybe I should come in tomorrow and sweet-talk young Hường." Mrs. Thân startled, threw the makeup box she was holding into Thân, "You dare. These guys really take advantage of every situation."

Thân grinned slyly. After parking the car in front of the house, he picked up the makeup box and handed it back to his wife. She went inside to prepare the evening meal, while he rushed off to his side job, fixing water pipes inside houses for some familiar clients or those recommended by acquaintances. Mrs. Thân had only taken a couple of steps when she turned back to remind her husband, "Later, on your way back, remember to stop and buy me a bag of potatoes. The 4.5-kilogram bag, priced at $2.15.

Thân hadn't had a chance to respond when his wife added with a firm tone, "Remember, it's the large 4.5-kilogram bag, priced at $2.15. Last time, you brought home a $3 bag. They were so expensive that they almost gave me a choke trying to eat them.

Thân shook his head, looking at his wife, "You've lost the charm of the Nail salon owner." Mrs. Thân puzzled, "What charm did I lose?" Thân grinned ear to ear recalling, "I heard people say that Nail salon owners are quite well-off. When they go out to eat, they order two lobster tails at once. Except for the days when there's grilled mackerel with soy sauce, then they would settle for one big lobster tail to go with the fish!"

Mrs. Thân scoffed at her husband, "Whom do you think I am saving money for? Isn't it for paying the university tuitions for our two kids? Thân, knowing better, accelerated the car away.

6. The princess at home

Mrs. Thân swiftly entered the house, making a beeline for the kitchen where she busied herself preparing the evening meal. As she sorted through spices for the dishes, her attention soon turned to baking cakes, a ritual she upheld twice a week for her children.

Initially, she noticed her two little ones were indifferent to eating fruits. In an attempt to entice them, she diligently peeled and arranged apples and oranges on the table each morning. When this tactic failed, she devised a plan to incorporate fruits into cakes. She crafted banana chiffon cakes infused with slices of apples or strawberries. Now, aware of the purported brain-boosting benefits of blueberries, Mrs. Thân purchased some for her youngest, Win.

However, Win's perception of blueberries shifted when he learned from his school teacher that they were a favorite food of forest bears, leading him to consider them dirty and unappetizing. Yet, once mixed into the cakes, his aversion dissolved. Despite acknowledging that cooking fruits might diminish their nutritional value, Mrs. Thân adopted a pragmatic stance: "Whether it's horizontally nutritious or vertically, it's still nutritious."

After the evening meal concluded and the utensils were set aside, Thân and her children settled into the plush cushioned chairs in front of the oversized TV screen occupying one corner of the room. As they awaited Mrs. Thân's company for a Vietnamese music program, Thân engaged the children in conversation about their day at school. With not more than a few words exchanged, Thảo invited her sibling to join her in the upstair room to explore a new video game.

Mrs. Thân emerged from the entertainment room and settled next to Thân, stretching her legs onto the low coffee table, leaning back with a sigh of relief. Observing her exhaustion, Thân promptly fetched half a basin of warm water from the kitchen and brought it for his wife to soak her feet.

Noticing Mrs. Thân's fatigue, Thân remarked, "You should teach our child how to cook so they can help you."

Mrs. Thân responded, "Let them have time for their study."

Thân pressed on, "Studying is one thing, but they should also assist with household chores."

She replied, "They're still young; making them do household chores seems harsh."

Thân countered, "Loving our child involves preparing them to live independently, like the customs of Canadians. I think that's beneficial."

Mrs. Thân disagreed, "Oh, come on, dear. Acting like Linda's couple next door, I can't do that. They're counting the days, waiting for their son to move out."

Thân nodded, "Yeah, they're a bit extreme. Last week, I met them outside in the garden, and they proudly announced that their son got his driver's license. Before I could congratulate them, they added, 'Now he can move out on his own.'"

Mrs. Thân expressed her confusion, "I really don't understand why they push their children away like that."

Thân concluded, "That's why everything should be done in moderation. Spoiling our child like you do, I think it's also too much." Mrs. Thân defended, "I want our children to enjoy their childhood fully. As implied in the song '60 Years of Life' by the composer Y Vân, 'Joyfulness comes only in the first 20 years of life.'" Thân shook his head, "I worry that you're taking on too much, my dear."

Mrs. Thân grew up akin to a princess, much like many fortunate children born into Vietnamese families. They were all the little princes and princesses of their parents, not because their parents were royalty or affluent enough to provide a regal lifestyle, but because their parents' hearts and immense sacrifices for them surpassed any golden throne or wealth.

"Focus on your studies for Mom; you don't need to worry about anything else," was the recurring advice Mrs. Thân received from her mother. Her mother managed everything at home, granting Mrs. Thân the time to dedicate herself to her studies. Unfortunately, those joyous days passed swiftly as the country became engulfed in deadly armed conflicts, between factions and ideologies, which directly or indirectly snatched away the most precious elements of Mrs. Thân's life. Her parents departed, one after the other, without a farewell.

Those who believe in the law of compensation wouldn't be surprised to observe how adversity contributed to shaping Mrs. Thân's survival instincts, aiding her in weathering numerous storms and emerging as a resilient woman embarking on a new life in a foreign land.

Throughout her arduous journey, Mrs. Thân kept the flame of her parents' love alive in her heart, akin to a lighthouse illuminating the path for her children. It served as a beacon, conveying to them that, despite the challenges, love still thrives in this world through her meticulous care. This, too, was Mrs. Thân's way of expressing profound gratitude towards her parents.

The couple sat before the TV, engrossed in a Vietnamese musical show from a recently rented videotape. It served as a delightful way to unwind after a long day of conversing in English, extending warm greetings to customers with phrases like 'Hello, how are you?' Additionally, they conversed in English between themselves, adhering to Mrs. Thân's rule to exhibit respect to their clientele.

On the screen, singer Thanh Tuyền graced the stage with each musical note, enveloped by a serene ambiance and palpable anticipation. As her voice soared, it seized the audience in a whirlwind, whisking them far beyond the horizon to a military outpost or a schoolyard amidst the season of red phoenix flowers. Her familiar voice summoned clouds, summoned rain, and transported wanderers' souls and bodies back to a homeland of yesteryears, evoking memories and tender sentiments.

In this manner, Mr. and Mrs. Thân immersed themselves in the performance, tracing each lyric and melody with keen attention, sometimes somber, sometimes jubilant, discerning the subtleties. If Thanh Tuyền's singing ensnared the souls of romantics, then the soothing voice of Hoàng Oanh gently released souls into the clouds, allowing the wind to carry them along with the music. It steered the vessel of memories against the current of time, navigating the alleys of the soul, evoking joy or sorrow, or listening to the whispers of love, arousing nostalgic childhood memories.

The wanderers sought solace in these overseas musical programs, aiming to rediscover familiar eyes, smiles, and to hear the voices of their youth through rhythmic songs resonating from the mountains, rivers, and waters of Vietnam. They sought reassurance that they still had each other, finding comfort in the knowledge that the descendants of the legendary Mother Âu Cơ endured.

"Okay, I have a solution now, my dear. Listen to me," Mrs. Thân's voice abruptly shattered her husband's reverie. Though Thân didn't comprehend his wife's intentions, he sensed she wasn't referring to the stage performance they were watching.

"What's this about? We're watching the show. Anything else can leave until later," he teased.

"I have a plan to address the issue of nail technicians competing for clients in the salon."

"We can't even enjoy the music together. I guess composer Song Ngọc was right: '*Oh, women are the pains*.'"

"Tomorrow, I propose holding a meeting to announce to everyone that we should discourage technicians from competing for clients in our salon. We're not singling anyone out."

Thân pondered, "That's a good idea. Speaking privately to Hường might offend her, leading to her resignation. It's better to appeal to everyone's self-awareness. Hopefully, those who realize their mistakes will rectify them."

"Exactly. It's a positive start," Mrs. Thân agreed.

Thân sighed and redirected his wife's attention, "Okay, it's comedy time, with our favorite comedian, let's watch it."

Having eagerly awaited for months to see comedian Kiều Oanh again, Mrs. Thân couldn't afford to miss it. Thân's joy surged as he exclaimed, "Oh, and Ngọc Đan Thanh is here too."

"I really admire her; not only does she sing beautifully, but she's also multi-talented. Can you guess what else she does?" Mrs. Thân inquired.

"Acting in plays?" Thân guessed.

"Correct, but there's another talent," she hinted.

"What talent?" Thân questioned.

"She does voice dubbing in the films we watch."

Thân recalled, "Oh, right. Her stage voice reflects the refined accent of old Saigon."

Mrs. Thân nudged her husband, prompting a sense of familiarity in him. Realizing she alluded to his past romantic interest with a similar voice, Thân decided to enjoy the play in peace and diverted the conversation, "I enjoy watching plays before bed. They help me sleep well."

"That's true. Science can explain that, you know," Mrs. Thân responded.

"I know. Research indicates that laughter triggers the release of hormones that reduce stress and boost happiness. That's why good sleep often follows," Thân explained.

"I've heard that even simulating a smile can trigger the release of these hormones, even without anything funny happening. How peculiar, isn't it?" she remarked.

The comedy play on stage had concluded, yet Mrs. Thân persisted in laughter, clutching her stomach. She leaned into her husband, patting his shoulder, while attempting to mimic a few pageant English phrases that the comedian had just sprinkled across the audience. Their banter was a playful fusion of Vietnamese and American humor.

Thân chuckled in tandem, laughter lines still ringing in his ears. He casually reached for the remote, silencing the TV without a word. Lifting his wife in his arms, he started toward the bedroom upstairs. However, before reaching the dining room, Mrs. Thân wriggled out of his embrace.

"Let me prepare lunch for our child, dear," she insisted.

She headed straight to the kitchen, crafting two sandwiches and washing two apples, neatly arranging them in lunch boxes for the children's school the next day. Thân sighed, his inner thoughts embracing him as he slowly ascended the stairs alone.

7. The fondue party

Close to twenty individuals, a mix of nail technicians, their children, and a few relatives, congregated at the Búp Măng (Bamboo Shoots) Nails salon for a lively Thai hot pot party hosted by 'Chef' Hường, with Mrs. Thân contributing high-quality seafood. Thân began spreading two green polyester tent cloths in the center of the floor, setting the stage for the festivities. Phượng, a new technician, knelt down attentively, smoothing them meticulously from the inside out.

Phượng dedicated her time to honing the art of nail painting using dry colored powder, known in the industry as 'Điếp,' a term derived from the English word 'Dip.' This method involves applying a base coat of glue to the nails and then immersing the fingertip into a jar of colored powder, ensuring the powder adheres to the nail. Typically, this process is repeated two or three times to achieve a vibrant and long-lasting color, resistant to chipping. Notably, this technique offers convenience over using 'Gel' since there's no need to wait for the color to dry under the UV lamp.

While Phượng was still mastering the 'Điếp' method, she overheard a colleague, who had started her career at the same time, learning the Acrylic powder technique at the neighboring salon, sparking her curiosity to learn more. Unlike the dry dipping technique, the Acrylic powder method involves using a brush to lift portions of the gel-like powder from the jar and applying it to the nail, then skillfully spreading it out. Consequently, this nail painting method is also known as 'Đắp bột' (Applying Acrylic powder) to differentiate it from the dry dipping technique.

Phượng looked at Mrs. Thân, her expression a blend of jest and earnestness.

"Mrs. Thân, when can you teach me the Acrylic powder application?" she inquired.

"Well, once you've mastered 'Điếp,' then we can delve into 'Đắp,'" Mrs. Thân replied with a smile.

Quang, rolling his eyes, playfully teased Phượng, "This little one doesn't even know how to walk yet and already wants to run."

Hường, a year older than Phượng, chimed in with sisterly advice, "If you're unsure, just ask. I remember a lady in the salon where I used to work; she claimed expertise in everything but often made mistakes. The customers never stopped complaining."

By now, all the party guests had gathered around, seated on the polyester sheets encircling the hot pot of soup amidst plates of seafood, bowls of vermicelli, and baskets of vegetables. Hường reached out to a kettle to pour more boiling water into the hot pot before continuing her story:

"Watching her apply the powder was comical. While most people delicately applied the powder, she would smear it everywhere. The salon owner finally told her to stick to regular nail polish, deeming the powder application too troublesome."

Quang erupted into laughter, "Her technique was more like pounding the powder rather than 'applying' it. If she encountered a difficult customer, she might get a 'pounding.'"

Hường added, "Indeed, for manicures, but with pedicures, you have to watch out not to get 'kicked.'"

Laughter echoed through the salon as Quang took a sip of beer, adopting a philosophical tone. "That's why our forefathers said, 'The nail profession requires a multitude of skills!' It encompasses all kinds of 'pounding' and 'kicking.'"

The group shared hearty laughter, reveling in the camaraderie of the moment.

Mrs. Thân chuckled at the remark, her laughter interrupted by concern about the direction of the conversation. Sensing Hường possibly teasing someone in the salon, she intervened with a gentle warning,

"Hey, hey, today is for stress relief. No shop talk, okay, guys?"

Quang, curious, responded, "We're just having a fun conversation."

"We have a saying, 'Too much anger leads to foolishness, and too much eating leads to loss of appetite.' But the saying misses one thing," Mrs. Thân remarked.

"What's that, Mrs. Thân?" Quang inquired.

"Excessive fun is not good either," she explained. "For now, the butt of a joke is with another store, but before we know it, it may turn toward us, and someone may take it personally. That's when trouble begins. You see?"

"A little teasing is also fun, Mrs. Thân. It's also a way to relieve stress," Quang countered.

"I know, here people say gentle teasing is a way to connect emotionally or build camaraderie. But if it goes too far and annoys others, it's not good. Everything has its limits," Mrs. Thân cautioned.

Mr. Thân, understanding his wife's point, quickly raised his beer, inviting Quang and everyone else,

"Bottoms up! The water is boiling. The soup is ready."

Everyone happily joined in, some raising beer bottles high, others lifting plastic cups filled with soft drinks, clinking them together. Hường stood up and removed the apron she wore while cooking. Mrs. Năm and Mrs. Thân were startled, staring at the elegant white lace dress reminiscent of Princess Diana strolling through the gardens at Buckingham Palace. Mrs. Năm pursed her lips and looked away. Mrs. Thân glanced at her husband, keeping an eye on him.

Before fully settling onto the floor, Hường swiftly picked up two thumb-sized large scallops, dipped them in the boiling water, and placed them in Đức's bowl. Đức, Mrs. Năm's son sitting next to her, was a medical student whom Mrs. Năm kept hidden so he could focus on his studies. To newcomers, it seemed like Mrs. Năm was a single mother. Even long-time acquaintances like Mr. and Mrs. Thân rarely had the chance to meet Đức. Yet, somehow, Hường had become acquainted with Mrs. Năm's son and acted very friendly. Mrs. Thân wondered about that. From then on, Mrs. Năm ate the hotpot as if she were taking bitter medicine, tasting only the bitterness of vegetables on her tongue.

Đức, served by the beautiful Hường, felt even happier, raising his chopsticks and picking up several pieces of vermicelli. Earlier, when the discussion revolved around nail techniques, Đức had a thought he wanted to contribute, but Mrs. Thân abruptly cut off the conversation. Sensing a somewhat subdued atmosphere at the party, Đức, after setting down his bowl, sought to initiate a conversation with Thân.

"Uncle, why don't you organize a workshop?" he proposed.

Thân wondered, "What kind of workshop, dear?"

"Last year, I attended a neuroscience workshop with my professor in Hawaii. I liked it a lot," Đức elaborated.

"What workshop was it?" Thân inquired.

"It was a neuroscience conference, Uncle," Đức clarified.

Thân discreetly glanced at his wife. Mrs. Thân understood her husband's implication: 'Mrs. Năm is pushing her son too hard in his studies, and he's becoming naive.' She quickly avoided her husband's gaze, fearing that Mrs. Năm might catch on to the signals exchanged between them. Thân looked at Đức sympathetically and replied,

"We do nails; what do we know about neuroscience to organize a workshop?"

Mrs. Thân nearly burst out laughing but managed to contain herself, narrowly avoiding squirting vermicelli out of her nose. Đức raised his hands in objection and explained,

"Not like that, Uncle. What I meant is that you could organize a workshop on Nails. Let nail technicians meet and exchange experiences in the profession. Earlier, I was impressed by all the nail techniques you have."

Thân nodded thoughtfully, "So that's how it is. It sounds like a good idea, but I wonder if anyone organizes a professional workshop like that."

"Yes, Uncle. That time, in the hotel where I stayed, there was another workshop for hairstylists. Reading their advertisement, I saw that besides technical issues, they also exchanged experiences in managing hair salons. Furthermore, there were many discussions about products related to hair care in the industry," Đức elaborated.

Thân looked at Đức in admiration, "Is that so? You're quite talented, and you have keen observation," he remarked, sharing a silent thought with his wife, 'The boy is really smart.' After a moment of contemplation, Thân looked at Đức with curiosity, "How do they organize such workshops, young man?"

"I think it requires an attractive venue, topics that many people in the industry are interested in, and famous, experienced speakers," Đức explained.

"But to have a good venue like Hawaii, it must cost a lot, right?" Thân queried.

"We need sponsors, Uncle. We need individuals or commercial establishments to support the workshop costs. In this case, we could ask companies that produce gel, color powder, or nail polish to help," Đức suggested promptly.

Mr. and Mrs. Thân found themselves intrigued by Đức's unique suggestion. Thân chuckled half-jokingly, "That's a brilliant idea. We could even organize it on a cruise or in other famous scenic places, gathering nail technicians from around the world, once a year."

Many people nodded in approval, accompanied by enthusiastic responses, "That sounds fun!" and "If there's such a workshop, I want to attend too. Traveling and learning more, plus meeting many colleagues."

Hường joyfully cheered, "Brother Thân, organize it! And take me along!"

The bright smile on Mrs. Thân's face suddenly disappeared unnoticed. Thân quickly intervened, lifting his beer can and inviting everyone, "Come on, come on, join in!"

8. The love bud

Leaving the Thai hotpot party, as soon as she arrived at her car in the parking lot, Mrs. Năm reproached Đức, "How many times have I told you to focus on your studies, but you never listen."

Đức was taken aback, "What happened, Mom?"

Mrs. Năm shook her head in frustration, "I told you to prioritize your education. Finish it first, secure a stable life before anything else."

Đức was surprised, assuming his mother knew about his secret relationship with Thảo. While Đức was contemplating an explanation, Mrs. Năm impatiently asked, "In just a few months, you'll be a certified doctor. Do you think you could marry a laborer?"

"Why do you hold such class discrimination, Mom?" Đức retorted.

"It's not me being feudal or class-oriented. Try to think if your grandma would consent to such a marriage?"

Coincidentally, as they were driving, they passed by a garbage truck parked on the side of the road. Đức pointed and asked Mrs. Năm, "Do you see that garbage truck? It passes by our house every week. There's a driver sitting in the front, and a young man perched on the back dock. Every time the truck stops in front of someone's house, he jumps down, lifts their trash bin, and empties it into the truck. He has to stand behind the garbage truck all day just to do that job."

"What's your point? Do you want to work as a garbage collector?" Mrs. Năm inquired.

"I just want to ask why the person doing that job has to be him and not me. Society needs garbage collectors, and if it's not him, then it should be me or someone else. Depending on circumstances or personal conditions, each person in the community takes on a specific task. No job is superior, and no job is inferior."

Mrs. Năm felt that her child had truly grown up. She understood what her child wanted to express. Parental love is profound, but when aimed too high, it is easy to fall into the traps of envy and jealousy, where in the eyes of parents, only their own child remains. All other children in the world are just weeds.

Đức, sensing his mother's silence, tentatively inquired, "Thảo is still studying; she's not working at a nail salon, Mom."

"I didn't mention Thảo, did I? I see Hường sitting right next to you, attentive and all," Mrs. Năm replied.

Đức sighed, relieved to unload a heavy burden. It turned out he had misunderstood Mrs. Năm's intention. "Hường already has a boyfriend, Mom. They're even planning their wedding. What were you talking about?"

"Oh, really?"

"That guy is my classmate. They're keeping it a secret. I just found out after accidentally meeting them in the hospital cafeteria a few weeks ago," Đức explained.

Mrs. Năm burst into laughter. "I apologize for the misunderstanding." In her heart, she also felt a light joy because this allowed her to learn more about her son. Despite living together for a long time, there were rare occasions for them to exchange or confide in each other.

Mrs. Năm tried to explain the seemingly disparaging words she blurted out in frustration regarding Hường. "I understand your point, and over the years living here, I've somewhat adopted the open-minded thinking of others. I never really thought about who you love or marry. But, in Hường's case, I think..."

Mrs. Năm thought for a moment, searching for a way to explain. "You're studying to become a doctor, so you probably know that sometimes our dislike for others is actually a reflection of our own self-hatred. Maybe I don't like Hường because she reminds me of myself in the past. From being a precious little flower to one day sitting on the roadside, wearing a conical hat to hide my face, washing dishes for others just to get a meal for the day."

"I understand, Mom," Đức replied.

"Also, as people often say here, every immigrant brings along a burden, whether it's the constraints of customs and traditions from their previous home or the personal sorrows in their hearts that force them to leave their homeland," Mrs. Năm reflected, her voice tinged with uncertainty.

Mrs. Năm hesitated before continuing,

"I'm the same. Every day here, I think about your father and your grandmother. I only wish for you to find happiness in the new land, and for your grandmother to be proud of you. Now that you've achieved success in your studies, my next worry is to find a decent place for your marriage. Only by achieving that goal would I consider fulfilling my last wish to make your father and grandmother happy."

Đức held his mother's hand, conveying both his comprehension of her predicament and a silent plea for her to desist from what appeared to be begging him. He dreaded the thought of losing the image of the mother he knew - a woman of strength and determination, who had triumphed over countless obstacles and adversities, many of which he had witnessed firsthand on numerous occasions.

Standing at a crossroads, Đức hesitated, uncertain whether it was the right moment to confide in his mother about his feelings for Thảo and the future plans they harbored in their hearts.

Not long ago, their paths crossed serendipitously, an encounter shaped, if one were to describe it indirectly, by Thảo's passion for music. Since ninth grade, Thảo has been actively engaged in community service activities to fulfill high school graduation requirements. In the inaugural year, Thảo joined an amateur music ensemble, entertaining the elderly at nursing homes every weekend. The ensemble, founded by a lawyer couple, also includes an accountant and a retired civil servant. They are proficient in various musical instruments, from horns to pianos and the ukulele. The lawyer's wife assumed the role of lead vocalist, infusing their performances with joy.

Blessed with a natural singing talent nurtured from a young age through avidly watching Vietnamese music videos and enthusiastically singing along with various artists, Thảo frequently participated in school cultural events, capturing the attention of a teacher who connected her with the volunteer music ensemble.

Driven by inherent compassion and the idealism of youth, after fulfilling her school's mandatory volunteer hours, Thảo expressed a desire to continue collaborating with the community service ensemble. Touched by her love for humanity, the ensemble proposed incorporating a Vietnamese song for Thảo to perform. Coincidentally, the Canadian-American civil servant, familiar with a piece by the renowned composer Phạm Duy - a song he had cherished since first hearing it performed by the esteemed singer Bạch Yến in an American troop's entertainment, led by the legendary entertainer Bob Hope aboard a U.S. Navy ship - suggested "Ngậm Ngùi" (Pity).

One day, in the lobby of the Red River nursing home, affectionately referred to as the 'Sông Hồng' nursing home by the Vietnamese expatriates because it reminds them of a historical river in their homeland, the elderly residents gathered closely in a semicircle in front of the band, with Thảo deeply immersed in her singing.

"The sunlight splits the afternoon in half
In the deserted garden, the virgin vine neatly arranges its leaves
A spider quickly spins threads of melancholy

My love, please sleep, as I fan gently here."
(Translated by someone.)

Thảo's eyes suddenly caught a familiar and endearing sight. In the back row of seats, a local woman, around her mother's age, sat hunched, delicately painting the nails of an elderly lady while she listened to the music.

After the singing session, Thảo approached the elderly lady, learning that her daughter often visited to take care of her nails. The elderly lady looked at Thảo with innocent eyes, proudly extending her hands in front of her, showcasing her freshly painted red nails. With a carefree smile, she proudly exclaimed, "Look at my new nails."

A shadow passed over the otherwise clear sky, and Thảo's heart sank as she realized that the elderly lady seemed to have lost awareness of her own identity. Yet, amidst the bitterness, there was sweetness in what the lady still held onto in her endless journey - an innocent smile and the sparkling eyes of a lost star, which Thảo believed would forever shine among the countless celestial lights illuminating the universe every night.

Thảo suddenly conceived the idea to join the compassionate journey of the kind-hearted woman, painting her mother's nails, to illuminate not just one star but many others that traverse the countless galaxies beyond endless space. Since then, every time she accompanied the volunteer band to bring joy to the nursing home, little Thảo always brought along a bottle of cherry-red nail polish to "beautify" the elderly who had no family to visit them.

Then, on a winter afternoon, the son of another nails technician, a medical student named Đức, equipped with a compassionate heart, visited the "Sông Hồng" nursing home. Đức came to share general medical knowledge about elderly healthcare with the residents.

Compared to what Đức hoped to contribute, he unexpectedly received much more. When Đức encountered Thảo, this meeting differed from the previous ones occasionally taking place at the nail salon. It seemed like the first time they discovered the encounter between two souls. If compassion brought the two young Vietnamese hearts together, then love deeply etched the image of the two in their tender hearts.

9. Running the family

On Tuesday, after the closure of Búp Măng (Bamboo Shoots) Nails, Thân wrapped up his lunch and summoned his wife to the family room for some Vietnamese music videos. Mrs. Thân declined, opting instead to head straight to the kitchen, murmuring, "I have to make some cakes." It was her usual sponge cake recipe, albeit this time with a new twist courtesy of a friend from the U.S. While Mrs. Thân busied herself in the kitchen, Thân settled into the family room, watching TV with their two children.

From the kitchen, Mrs. Thân called out, "Honey, how much is half a pint in liters?"

Thân teased her, "Why is it that you can remember all the food prices at the stores so well, but when it comes to the conversion of American measurement units, you always give up?"

Undeterred, Mrs. Thân, holding a cup of water, eyes fixed on the recipe sheet, retorted, "Do you want cake this afternoon or not? Answer quickly so I can get it done."

"Wait a moment. Let me check the notebook," Thân responded.

Accustomed to his wife's frequent queries about unit conversions, Thân had diligently recorded conversion formulas in a small notebook hidden among Vietnamese magazines scattered on the coffee table. As he searched, Mrs. Thân shifted the conversation, "We haven't seen Đức, Mrs. Năm's son, for a while. He looks like a handsome young man now. Don't you think?"

Thân, finding the conversion numbers, replied, "Spouses really do have telepathy! I was just thinking about him too." Glancing at Thảo, their daughter engrossed in TV with her brother, he casually hinted to his wife, "Looks like you want to be an in-law with Mrs. Năm."

Mrs. Thân replied in coded language, ensuring Thảo wouldn't catch on to their discussion about her future, "How could we have missed this case? We look right and left, and it's right in front of us, and we didn't see it."

Finally, Thân found the unit conversion number and informed his wife, "Let's say it's approximately a quarter of a liter." Reflecting on Thảo's situation, he suggested, "How about next Tuesday, we invite the two of them, Mother and Son, to our house for a 'bánh xèo' (Vietnamese pancakes) meal."

"Sure, that would work," Mrs. Thân agreed.

Half an hour later, six baking molds were filled with batter mixed with blueberries. Mrs. Thân placed them in the oven before stepping out to the living room to watch TV. Thân, aware of his role, stood up, preparing to head to the market. Typically, he and his wife went grocery shopping on Tuesdays when the Nails salon was closed. However, this morning, due to being busy driving to various places to buy ingredients for Thai hotpot, they had to postpone part of their weekly grocery shopping for the family.

Mrs. Thân eased herself onto the long cushioned chair by the coffee table and then turned to her daughter, "Thảo, go upstairs and bring down two baskets of dirty clothes for Mom. I'll be doing the laundry tonight. Washing clothes at night is more cost-effective on electricity."

After addressing Thảo, she turned to Thân, who was awaiting instructions, "Could you bring down the stack of advertising flyers I left on the TV stand?" Mrs. Thân picked up a pen from the coffee table, circled the advertised items she wanted Thân to buy, and jotted down the quantity for each item. Not entirely reassured and fearing that her husband might buy the wrong things or forget something, she tore a corner of the advertising paper with a blank space to list the needed food and spices, handing it back to Thân to take to the market.

As Thân turned away, Mrs. Thân reminded him, "Remember to buy the type of coriander we always eat. Be careful not to get the Italian coriander with larger leaves. If you're unsure, just smell it. Italian coriander has a sharper scent."

Thân walked to the front door, hunched over, busy tying his shoelaces, when his wife approached and added, "Don't forget to drive to the market farther from our house for lettuce. They have a lower price, 3 bundles for $2.50. The store near us also has a sale, but it's more expensive, 2 bundles for $1.75."

Thân mumbled, "Uh-huh, okay," enduring the familiar chorus in his ears. However, as he stepped out to the car, a question lingered in his mind: How could his wife glance at the price list and instantly discern which items were cheap or expensive without needing a handheld calculator like him?

Mrs. Thân turned back into the house, making her way to the laundry room, where she sorted out various types of clothes that could be washed together in one cycle. Her hands were busy with the immediate task, but her mind was preoccupied with calculating future events, revolving around the upcoming Vietnamese pancake party to entertain Mrs. Năm and her son. In reality, in the Thâns' minds, it was a son-in-law introduction gathering. The couple wanted to create an opportunity to assess the future son-in-law, to see if he was worthy of their daughter Thảo.

Returning from the market, Thân clumsily carried two baskets of groceries into the kitchen, placing them on the floor next to the three-door refrigerator. Mrs. Thân eagerly rushed to greet her husband, not with a hug or a whispered "I love you" in his waiting ears, but with the goal of searching for the grocery bills and meticulously reviewing the prices of each item. She checked whether her husband had bought them at the advertised 'on sale' prices. If so, she would proudly declare... there would be a reward. The nature of the reward remained unknown, but in the world of married couples, such mysteries are best left untouched.

10. Searching for root

After returning from the market and storing all the groceries in the refrigerator, it marked the end of a long day for Mr. and Mrs. Thân. Without delay, they made their way eagerly to the television in the family room, a moment they had anticipated throughout the day and for the past two weeks. It had been since they finished watching the previous video tape from an overseas music entertainment center.

Vietnamese video tapes from abroad are meticulously produced and highly valued, making their timely release a challenge for compatriot fans like Mr. and Mrs. Thân. Once one video ended, the couple eagerly awaited the next, a sentiment echoed by many who visited the video shops over the weekend.

Relaxing on the sofa, Mr. and Mrs. Thân settled in. Thân reached for the coffee table, grabbed the remote control, and eagerly started the Vietnamese music video tape.

Four eager eyes remained fixed on the TV screen, as if attempting to escape the constraints of today, yesterday, and even tomorrow, immersing themselves in the music's lyrics and rediscovering cherished memories. They sought melodies hidden in the corners of their souls, originating from the lullabies of yesteryears to the lively voices of children outside in the alley.

The bridge to the past unfolded not only through familiar and intimate sounds but also through images of ripe golden rice fields, clusters of green bamboo, a rickety bamboo bridge spanning a small stream, atop gently drifting water lilies.

Suddenly, Thân pressed the remote control button, freezing the TV screen at a familiar city scene. He urgently called out to his son playing a video game upstairs,

"Nghĩa, come down here and watch this. It's fantastic."

Thân patiently urged his busy son; Nghĩa reluctantly paused the video game he was engrossed in to satisfy his father's request. Before Nghĩa even reached the bottom of the stairs, Thân pointed at the screen and exclaimed,

"Look, it's a cyclo!"

"Cool," Nghĩa responded in colloquial language, expressing delight or fascination with something new. Thân enthusiastically pointed out different parts of the cyclo, reminiscing about the past,

"When I was little, every time I had the chance to go to the market with your grandmother, I loved sitting on this footrest here. I would spread my arms wide, gripping both sides of the fender, pretending I was steering the vehicle."

Nghĩa widened his eyes and exclaimed,

"Cool."

Thân took a breath and continued his story,

"Those cyclo riders always wore shorts and conical hats, just like that. While waiting for passengers, they often sought out the shade of a large tree, then climbed into the passenger seat for a good nap."

Nghĩa responded again,

"Cool."

Faced with his son's indifferent attitude, Thân gradually realized that certain memories from their homeland, whether joyful or sorrowful, would forever remain personal. After his son went back upstairs, Mr.

and Mrs. Thân resumed immersing themselves in their private world through lively song and dance performances.

Later on, it was Mrs. Thân's turn to brighten up. She called Thảo downstairs,

"Come see your mother's school from back in the day."

"Mom's school is so beautiful," Thảo responded.

Mrs. Thân added, "Back then, I also wore a white 'áo dài' (Vietnamese long tunic) and a palm-leaf hat to go to school, just like those student girls."

"So beautiful," Thảo exclaimed.

Mrs. Thân urged, "Take a closer look, each girl even had the school's emblem pinned on the chest of her 'áo dài.'"

"Yes, I see."

After saying that, Thảo ran back upstairs to continue her interrupted phone conversation with her friend.

Mrs. Thân and her husband were taken aback by the seemingly hesitant attitude of their two children. Resignedly, they turned back to the stage, retreating into their own private world from a distant time. Immersed in memories amidst the myriad sparkling lights, they tried to find solace through familiar musical notes reminiscent of the cradle of their early years. They eagerly embraced the shared glances and empathetic smiles from the screen, as if they had known these people for a long time, as since the time they were born. The singers, though possibly strangers, except for their familiar voices and singing, now appeared through the TV screen, entering the living rooms of each overseas Vietnamese family as symbols of an era. Their presence, whether in the simple 'áo bà ba', typically country girl's attire with a shoulder-slung scarf, or in the elegant flowing 'áo dài', always exuded the complete style of a time when wanderers like the Thâns could easily recognize themselves, rediscovering their own essence.

These singers are faithful messengers of the legendary homeland, carrying with them the entirety of their native land where the sound of bamboo clashing and the rustling of palm leaves echo. The sounds of cheering in watering the rice fields, the times of abundant rain and the harmony of the wind, mingling with the sounds of sorrow during droughts and the annual floodwaters. They bring with them the laughter of reunions and the tears of partings. The joy of family gatherings blends with the sadness of bidding farewell to a doomed love.

Mrs. Thân suddenly exclaimed with joy, "There's Khánh Ly too!"

Thân, eyes glued to the TV, replied, "Yeah, it's been a while since we last saw her."

"You mentioned meeting her once, right?" Mrs. Thân asked.

"Yeah, that time. After performing for the soldiers, while the whole band was waiting for the plane back to Saigon, I saw her playing a card game with some officers."

Khánh Ly, a renowned singer, is an icon of her era, particularly through the songs she interpreted in the genre known as 'anti-war music' by composer Trịnh Công Sơn. In the midst of war, Khánh Ly may not have sung what people wanted to hear; instead, she voiced the inner thoughts of conscience. While her voice may not be resonant of a golden oriole whispering words of love in the waiting ears of a soldier at an outpost, it carries warmth and sincerity, with enough passion but not devoid of reasons to express the heartfelt sentiments of a sister, a daughter, in a feuded family. By chance of history, she possesses a voice, uniquely 'Khánh Ly,' that penetratingly conveys the deep struggles hidden within Trịnh's music.

Listening to Khánh Ly sing feels like sitting alone in a "small home,"[3] sipping sticky rice wine, feeling the warmth of the alcohol gradually infused into the body, sensing the sweetness of glutinous rice,

---

[3] From the song titled "Đi Tìm Quê Hương" by Trịnh Công Sơn.

savoring the strong taste of fermentation. It allows one to hear the whispers within the heartfelt narratives about human fate and the plight of the homeland, amidst the sound of bombs echoing daily in the cultivated fields.

After Khánh Ly's performance, the program hosts introduced the next young singer. It was already late, so Mrs. Thân urged Thân to turn off the TV. They needed rest for another day in the overseas land. As they ascended the stairs to the bedroom, the lingering echo of the music followed Mrs. Thân, prompting her to contrast between the old music, from Vietnamese songs that she dearly missed, and the new songs written by overseas Vietnamese artists.

"Why can't I appreciate new music written overseas? It sounds more like a conversation," she remarked.

Thân pondered, "New things must come for there to be old ones, dear."

"That may be true, but music should have melody and rhythm," she insisted.

"I think new music also has its own melody and rhythm. It's just that our ears are not accustomed to it, but it may appeal to many others, especially the younger generation," he explained.

"I have tried to listen to new music a few times, but just can't get used to it!"

"People say music reflects the emotions and thoughts of a community. Think about it, the large community growing up abroad has experiences different from those of previous generations in Vietnam. That's why today's music has to be different from the music of the past," he concluded.

Mrs. Thân playfully teased her husband, "So you're saying in the future, we'll get to hear traditional Vietnamese opera in English or French?"

"Yeah, I've heard people try to do that, but that's just a jest. I believe our creative musicians have rich imaginations. They will continue to explore new melodies and rhythms that better suit the emotions and lifestyles of people abroad, especially in a multicultural environment like here," he explained.

Mrs. Thân reflected, "Actually, if that happens, it would be great. Regardless of how good our old music is, every week I still look forward to finding something new and exciting to listen to."

Thân winked and said, "Whether it's new or old music, as long as it sounds good and makes you forget everything in the world, falling asleep until morning, then it's good music."

"Do you think every time we listen to music, we would sleep better?" she asked.

"Of course. Music has the power to soothe the soul and help us relax a lot," he replied.

"I heard some people even sing or play music for their babies while they're still in the womb," she added.

"I've heard that too. Science suggests that unborn babies in the womb can recognize their mother's voice or familiar melodies in music they frequently hear," he remarked.

Thân contemplated, nodding his head as he recalled the lyrics, 'I love the voice of my homeland from the moment I was born, ...,' from the song "Tình Ca" by composer Phạm Duy. He agreed the composer wasn't exaggerating in saying:

"*The voice of my homeland, the voice of my mother since the cradle*

In an instant, a thousand years become the voice of my heart, oh my country." (Translated by someone.)

These heartfelt lyrics, deeply rooted in their essence, resonate even more profoundly with overseas Vietnamese like Mr. and Mrs. Thân.

In a foreign land, when Vietnamese people eagerly await each day, anticipating each week to reconnect with Vietnamese music, those encounters go beyond merely appreciating scenes of the past, listening to familiar voices, or glimpsing familiar shadows. Instead, they serve as a journey to rediscover their roots, a quest to satisfy the primal urges of humanity, seeking peace and tranquility, lost within the womb of time.

11. Matchmaking

The eagerly anticipated week flew by swiftly. Mrs. Năm brought her son to the home of Mr. and Mrs. Thân to attend the 'Bánh xèo' (Vietnamese sizzling pancake) party. Mrs. Thân emphasized the importance of consuming 'bánh xèo' hot, almost directly from the pan, so she waited for the guests to arrive before beginning to prepare the pancakes. Upon arrival, Mrs. Năm insisted on assisting Mrs. Thân in the kitchen, while Đức sat at the dining table conversing with Thân.

Thân graciously opened a bottle of beer for Đức, saying, "Have a little to enjoy yourself. Having some beer to accompany 'bánh xèo' makes it more delightful." After clinking glasses, Thân, with a warm smile, turned to Đức and began to inquire, "Are you studying to become a doctor? You're quite talented. When do you expect to graduate?"

"I consider my studies complete. Currently, I am interning at the hospital under a doctor before I can obtain my professional license," replied Đức.

Without hesitation, Thân got to the point, "So, the studying part is practically finished. When do you plan to invite your 'aunt and uncle' here for the wedding feast?"

The ears of the aspiring doctor tinged slightly red, perhaps from the unfamiliarity of drinking beer or possibly due to the abruptness of Thân's question. Đức awkwardly smiled, his gaze shifting to the empty plate awaiting the 'bánh xèo', and hesitantly responded with a shy "Yes."

Mrs. Năm, bustling in the kitchen, eagerly brought a plate of freshly steaming 'bánh xèo' for Thân. He graciously thanked Mrs. Năm, and at that moment, he noticed Thảo and Nghĩa descending from upstairs. He called out, "Thảo, come sit next to Đức and have a chat, and Nghĩa, come sit next to your mom's seat at the end of the table."

The mother hen suddenly felt the shadow of a hawk circling down from the sky to snatch her chick. Mrs. Năm suddenly realized the true purpose of today's 'bánh xèo' party. They wanted to lure her son, 'the doctor', in. From that moment, her demeanor became noticeably cold. She spoke little, smiled sparingly, maintaining only the minimum social courtesy. Inside, she burned with impatience, waiting for the party to end so she could have a 'talk' with her son at home.

Mrs. Năm had known Thảo since she was a child. 'Aunt Năm' often painted Thảo's nails whenever she visited the nail salon. Thảo had a naturally honest and cheerful disposition, so in Aunt Năm's eyes, she was always the little Thảo from years past. That's why Mrs. Năm had let her guard down, and the price she had to pay today was unwittingly placing her son in the claws of the hawk. Thảo had blossomed into a beautiful and charming young woman, and despite Mrs. Năm's affection for her, she was angered by the scheming of Thảo's parents trying to capture her son's heart.

Mrs. Thân finished frying the last 'bánh xèo', walked over to the dining table still catching her breath, but still smiled and greeted Đức. Then, she turned to Thảo and asked, "It's been a long time since you two had the chance to meet, hasn't it?"

Thảo shyly lowered her head. Đức avoided Mrs. Thân's scrutinizing gaze, glancing at Thảo for help. Seeing Thảo still not responding, Đức hesitated, "Well, um... not that long, actually." Mrs. Năm was surprised by her son's answer. 'Do these two have a secret relationship?' she thought. Just as Mrs. Thân burst into laughter,

"Oh, I forgot. You two just met a few days ago at the Thai hotpot party, not that long ago at all."

Mrs. Năm breathed a sigh of relief. Đức smiled to navigate through the situation, waiting for the right moment to inform both families about his relationship with Thảo. Although Đức and Thảo had been discussing it for a week, both were hesitant about facing potential unfavorable reactions from the adults.

Thảo was determined to follow her parents' wishes and continue pursuing higher education, adhering to their plans. While Đức had managed to casually inquire about Mrs. Năm's opinions on his future, he still wasn't sure about his mother's stance on Thảo's case.

After the party, Đức drove his mother home. The mother and son sat silence in the family room for a long while. Mrs. Năm sat next to Đức, looking out of the window, contemplating whether she should honestly tell her son about the purpose of their upcoming trip to Vietnam for the Tết (Vietnamese New Year) holiday. Speaking up might risk him canceling the trip. Yet, not speaking might lead him to blame her for not being truthful, an attitude instilled in him by his parents since childhood. As for Đức, he was torn about whether it was the right time to discuss his relationship with Thảo with his mother, a relationship he hoped would eventually lead to marriage.

The mother and son, each looking out in different directions, shared the same emotion - worries about the potential loss of something precious within their hearts. Mrs. Năm did not want to lose her only son, and Đức feared being separated from his first love. Happiness is always fragile, a consciousness engraved in human genes through countless generations witnessing the transient nature of joy and the inevitability of parting in human life.

In the end, Mrs. Năm decided to be honest with Đức to maintain trust in their relationship and also because her motherly intuition suggested that if she didn't speak up now, it might be too late. She hesitated and said, "You know, even though you excel in your studies and have become somebody in society, but at home, don't forget that you still have to show respect to the elders."

"What do you want to say, Mom?"

"Well, it's about your marriage. It's not that we're living abroad now, and '*having our own feathers*', we can do anything we like. This time when we go back to Vietnam, let your grandmother find a wife for you there to make her happy, my dear."

"I love Grandma, but the decision about my marriage should be mine."

"Here, we don't really know who is who, dear."

"I find everyone in our Vietnamese community here to be good. They all work hard, provide for their families, and care for their children's education. Many even take care of their relatives back in Vietnam as well."

Đức suddenly wanted to seize the opportunity to probe his mother's thoughts about Thảo and added,

"Like Aunt Thân's family. You also like Aunt Thân, right?"

"I know," she replied.

Mrs. Năm, in a contemplative tone, tried to persuade her son, "Have you heard some compatriots often complain 'After coming here, people think we are all sardines in the same can'? The complainers think that when they were in Vietnam, they were different from all others because they were wealthier, had a higher status, or some noble title. I don't like such an arrogant attitude. However, objectively speaking, here, nobody really knows each other's backgrounds or social status. Therefore, if you want to build lasting friendships, you need to be cautious and learn a bit about their past."

"Here is a land of immigrants, Mom. Should I investigate the roots of my friends from Uganda, Italy, or Poland who come here to study?"

"They are foreigners. I'm talking about among our Vietnamese people here."

Đức looked at his mother with a sympathetic look but couldn't help but laugh at the ironic and teasing thought.

"So, for people like us, we need to investigate three generations of family history. But for those from other countries, we don't need to, right, Mom?"

Mrs. Năm lowered her arms, her gaze drifting into the undefined space. Đức suddenly felt regretful for his seemingly trivial comment, realizing it may have underestimated a matter that was weighing heavily on his mother's mind. He tried to explain,

"I was just joking. In reality, did you know, Canada's over a hundred years of nation-building experience shows that the abilities and determination of each individual coming here are what matters, not their family history or lineage."

"I know. But it's different for our Vietnamese people."

Đức was perceptive enough to pick up a signal in the three words 'our Vietnamese people' that his mother had mentioned twice. He looked at his mother with compassion. Even though those people she referred to were half a world away, she still felt bound by the common values she once shared with them. Young Đức expressed his sentiments,

"The older I get, the more I admire you, Mom. I don't know where you find the extraordinary strength to go from being the wife of an officer one day to selling goods and carrying the family burden the next, even having to sit on the roadside to wash dishes and earn enough to feed the family."

Mrs. Năm looked at her son without blinking, astonished by the heartfelt words coming from the depths of his heart. These were words she had never heard and never expected. Until now, even though to many patients in the hospital, Đức might be their friendly 'doctor', to her, he was always a child in need of a mother's protection.

Đức looked at his mother, searching for comforting words,

"Yet, never have I seen you suffer as much as now. It's all just to make Grandma happy, and deep down, you also wish for my happiness."

Tears welled up in Mrs. Năm's eyes, the creases between her brows unable to conceal the emotions that suddenly flew off her face as the dawn broke after a long night of contemplation. She hugged her son tightly in her arms.

"Mom knows, my dear. You always understand mom."

Though there was no agreement between mother and son, both wanted to conclude the conversation at a point where both were content with the present and hoped for their borrowed moments of happiness to last forever. Both shared the anxious feeling that the meeting of the minds may still be a far distant on the road ahead. For Đức, going from understanding his mother to envisioning marrying someone he doesn't love was a step too far. For Mrs. Năm, empathy for her son might not be enough to break her free from the age-old constraints of ingrained customs.

12. Picking a grandson-in-law

The 'Bánh xèo' party appeared to be making no progress, judging by the indifferent expression and demeanor of Mrs. Năm. Thân pondered whether he should seek assistance from his mother in Vietnam. Across the ocean, the voice of Mrs. Sáu resonated:

- Hello!

- Is that you, Mom? I'm here.

- Yes, it's me.

- How are you, Mom?

- I'm fine, dear. And how are your spouse and children over there?

- We're all fine, Mom. How's the time over there now?

- It's noon, dear. I've just finished my lunch and I'm sitting outside enjoying the cool breeze.

- It's already midnight here, Mom.

After the familiar, albeit costly refrain over the long-distance telephone line, spanning from Canada to Vietnam, Mrs. Sáu had a 'case' she wanted to share with Thân.

"Do you remember Uncle Hai and Aunt Hai in Đa Kao?"

"Yes, I remember, Mom. Uncle Hai works as the librarian. Every time he visits dad, he brings a bunch of books for me to read."

"Yes, that's right. He has been a close friend of your father since they were in the countryside."

"Why are you mentioning Uncle Hai, Mom?"

"I don't know if Thảo remembers."

"Little Thảo probably doesn't remember him. She was too young when we met him."

"I want to talk about Aunt Hai, dear. Back then, whenever she came to our house with Uncle Hai, she used to hold Thảo in her arms, caressing her affectionately. Since she had a son, she really wanted a daughter."

Thân patiently listened to his mother's "old stories," refraining from urging her to get to the point, despite the ringing of the long-distance phone charges echoing in his head. It cost $5.50 for the first 3 minutes of conversation and subsequently 75 cents per minute. Although it may not seem like much, compared to Thân's initial income as a worker with the broom manufacturer when he first arrived in Canada, the phone bill for half an hour of talking to Mrs. Sáu was equivalent to what he earned after a full day of hard work in the factory.

After some circling around, Mrs. Sáu finally broached her topic:

"So, since the time you guys talked about Thảo having a boyfriend over there, it got me worried. I asked Aunt Hai to help us find a husband for her."

Thân tried to play it cool,

"She's still too young; let her focus on her studies first. Don't worry about these things. It's too early, Mom."

"Well, I'm just keeping an eye on it; no rushing or anything."

Saying is one thing, but inside Thân couldn't help but be curious to know more,

"Did Aunt Hai find any suitable matches, Mom?"

"Yes, there is one, and the family is quite well-off. They are looking for a wife for their son who just graduated from a university in the United States. Aunt Hai plans to introduce them to us so we can get acquainted and for them to have the opportunity to meet Thảo."

Hearing this, Thân was eager to learn more,

"Did you meet them yourself, Mom?"

"I had Aunt Hai take me to their house to check it out. The parents seem kind and gentle."

"Is their family background alright, Mom?"

"Yes, but it doesn't look promising, dear."

"Why, Mom?"

"I went to their house around noon, and coincidentally, I saw a young man riding a Honda motorcycle as he arrived. He had sunglasses on and was wearing a half-open shirt. When he saw me, he nodded and went straight to the backyard."

"Who is he, Mom?"

"He's the younger brother of the engineer in the U.S.."

"Really, Mom? What about your potential grandson-in-law? Did you see his pictures?"

"I didn't bother looking, dear. I think I have seen enough. Such a rebellious 'cowboy' style put me off."

"Mom, you're talking about the younger brother in Vietnam or the older one in the U.S.?"

"Well, I'm talking about the younger brother here," clarified Mrs. Sáu.

Thân was merely asking for the sake of conversation; he knew his mother too well. When seeking a potential grandson-in-law, it was necessary to scrutinize not just the interested individual but also his entire family. Thân teased his mother,

"Finding a suitable grandson-in-law that meets all your criteria must be tough, right Mom?"

"It's not that I'm being difficult, but the character of the children reflects the family's upbringing, dear. Seeing the younger brother here like that, I don't know how the older one is over there," Mrs. Sáu explained.

At the end of their conversation, Thân set aside the phone, lost in contemplation about his daughter's future.

13. The Difficult Words

This morning, after leaving the shop in Mrs. Năm's care, Mrs. Thân drove directly to Nghĩa's school for the end-of-term meeting with his teacher. It was a session where teachers and parents convened to discuss the students' progress and development both academically and at home.

Mrs. Thân felt reassured upon hearing the teacher praise Nghĩa for his excellent attitude towards learning, his love for reading books, and his high grades in various subjects. However, a humorous yet frustrating incident awaited her, making her eager to return home and address her husband.

Thân had been occupied with urgently fixing a leaky water pipe at a customer's house, which prevented him from accompanying Mrs. Thân to the school meeting. Upon returning home later in the day, he settled into the family entertainment room, playing a Vietnamese music video on the VCR.

As soon as Mrs. Thân stepped inside, she burst into laughter, surprising her husband. He asked, "What's making you so happy?"

Attempting to stifle her laughter, Mrs. Thân replied, "How could I be happy? It's all your fault that I was scolded at our son's school today."

Perplexed, Thân inquired, "What did I do to deserve being scolded?"

"Our son told his teacher that Vietnamese people, including you, don't know how to 'love.'"

Thân burst into laughter, unaware of the context of his child's story but finding it a perfect opportunity to tease his wife. "I already have two children, how can I not know 'love'?" he joked.

Mrs. Thân grabbed a cushion and playfully smacked him with it, trying to contain her laughter as she retorted, "Oh, come on, don't be so naughty. They meant 'love' as in affection, not your 'sinful' stuff."

It took more than three minutes for Mrs. Thân to stop laughing and finally share the beginning and end of Nghĩa's story with Thân.

During the 'interview' session, the teacher mentioned that one day she asked the students in the class to hug their parents when they got home and say, 'I love you, Mom and Dad.'

The next day, when the teacher asked how it went, Nghĩa said he forgot to do what the teacher instructed. When asked why, Nghĩa replied, "Because Vietnamese people don't say 'love,' so I forgot."

The teacher burst into laughter as she recounted the story to Mrs. Thân. She mentioned that she then asked Nghĩa, "So what do Vietnamese people say?"

Nghĩa confidently replied, "Vietnamese people only say 'Study.'"

It was Thân's turn to laugh heartily with his wife. A few minutes later, he pointed at his wife, blaming her, "It's because of you, not anyone else. Every day you keep telling the little one to study, study, study endlessly."

His wife defended herself, "As if you didn't do the same."

"Well, people do remind their kids to study, but there's a time for it, not anytime of the day."

Mrs. Thân attempted to turn the tables on her husband, saying, "It's also because of you."

Thân, puzzled, asked, "How is it my fault?"

"You never say 'I love you' every day, like those Canadian husbands do. That's why our child has never heard 'love' in this house!"

Sensing the shift in the conversation and not wanting to stir up trouble, Thân quickly changed the subject, "Earlier, I stopped by the music rental place to check. Luckily, there are new video tapes now. Do you want to watch?"

Unexpectedly, married life revealed that Thân, in addition to his primary and secondary careers, also possessed a talent for diversion!

14. From setback to comeback

Mrs. Thân scheduled an early appointment with Phượng at the nail salon to address a customer complaint about her recent nail treatment. Three days prior, Phượng had performed the service, but the customer experienced peeling in certain areas. Mrs. Thân speculated that the salon's bustling atmosphere that day might have led Phượng to rush, resulting in errors. While awaiting the customer's arrival, Mrs. Thân inquired,

"How many layers did you apply during the acrylic nail procedure?"

"Three layers, sister."

"Did you allow each layer to dry adequately before applying the next? Improper drying can lead to premature peeling."

"Yes, sister. I remember your instruction, and I ensured proper drying time."

"Are her nails in good condition? Sometimes, nails with a pronounced upward curve on both sides pose challenges in acrylic application. Without precision, acrylic may accumulate in the center, causing thickness and longer drying times."

"Is that the case, sister? I'll be mindful of it next time."

"One more point of caution: after applying acrylic to the nail tips, lightly tap the brush to remove excess acrylic."

"Just a gentle tap, sister?"

"Indeed, this step is crucial. Excessive tapping can lead to acrylic buildup at the tips, resulting in thick layers prone to smudging, especially for active individuals."

Promptly at the appointed time, Mrs. Thân welcomed the customer warmly and apologized sincerely. After introducing the customer to Phượng, Mrs. Thân briefly inspected workstations for cleanliness. At Quang's station, she queried,

"Where's your disinfectant?"

Mrs. Thân emphasized the importance of keeping disinfectant water accessible on the table for customer reassurance. Quang gestured to a shelf below the table,

"I keep it there."

"I've reminded you to keep it visible. Customers need to see it for peace of mind."

"I apologize, sister. I was concerned about a talkative customer's gestures knocking it over, so I placed it below."

"I almost believed you had a drinking habit!"

Mrs. Thân jested, reaching for towels for the customer. Despite being laundered, the towels remained unfolded due to Mrs. Thân's early departure to take Nghĩa to his music class.

The salon wasn't particularly busy. Mrs. Năm stood near the reception counter, gazing towards the entrance with a sense of unease lingering in her heart due to her distant demeanor at Mrs. Thân's 'bánh xèo' party the previous day. Quickly, she pivoted towards the laundry room, using the excuse of folding towels to mend the rift.

"I'm sorry I had to leave early yesterday. An urgent matter came up, and I couldn't stay to help with the dishes," she apologized.

Mrs. Thân secretly welcomed this explanation, relieved to have clarity regarding Mrs. Năm's behavior. Responding warmly, she said, "No worries at all. I'm glad you could join us. Besides, we usually just use the dishwasher for a pile of dishes."

During their private conversation yesterday, Mrs. Năm became aware of Đức's desire to discuss her attitude towards Thảo's family. The covert glances shared between the affectionate duo at the party certainly hadn't escaped the vigilant gaze of Mother Hen, who always kept a watchful eye on her child.

Today, however, Mrs. Năm felt more at ease after sharing her feelings with her son. She could now contemplate her child's future with a clearer mind. Initiating the conversation, she inquired, "So, Thảo has graduated. What are her plans now?"

"She's aiming for the University of Manitoba, sister," Mrs. Thân replied proudly.

"Quite impressive! What field is she interested in?" Mrs. Năm asked.

"She's leaning towards Science," Mrs. Thân responded.

Before Mrs. Năm could interject, Mrs. Thân seized the opportunity to probe her counterpart's thoughts,

"She also aspires to be a doctor like your son. But Thân mentioned how rigorous medical school can be; not everyone who applies gets accepted."

Mrs. Năm offered her advice, saying, "Let your daughter follow her passion. Thảo was an outstanding student in high school, after all."

Smiling, Mrs. Thân replied, "Thank you. Thảo mentioned that her backup plan is to become a pharmacist. Her friends jokingly suggested that if she can't become a doctor, she can always marry one. One spouse diagnoses, the other dispenses medicine - a perfect match, they say."

Mrs. Năm, taken aback, quickly signaled a cautious message to the 'bride family'...

"Are you planning to visit Vietnam for the Tết festival? If so, we should meet up for some fun. Đức's Aunt is urging me to bring him back for an official meeting with the family of the girl she found," she inquired Mrs. Thân.

Maintaining a calm demeanor, Mrs. Thân responded, "Is that so, sister? Congratulations to him. Now that he's done with his studies, it's time to think about finding a wife for him. You're truly blessed."

"Thank you. Blessings are not something I see; all I see is endless worry. When the child was young, I worried about his education; as he grows up, I worry about his future," Mrs. Năm lamented.

From outside, Quang's voice echoed, "There are customers, ladies! Two or three of them."

Mrs. Năm urged Mrs. Thân to attend to the customers while she stayed behind to finish folding the remaining towels.

Throughout the morning, Mrs. Thân had been awaiting her husband's arrival at the salon to share the 'hot news'. At lunchtime, Thân finally entered the office, finding Mrs. Thân preparing instant noodles. She waved him over, speaking quietly,

"Mrs. Năm just mentioned that this Tết, she'll take Đức home to prepare for his wedding," she disclosed.

Thân chuckled, "I thought you had something important. About him and Thảo, we were just kidding around."

"If you feel disappointed, just say so, you know," Mrs. Thân teased.

"Tonight, I'll call Mom," Thân declared.

"What for?" Mrs. Thân inquired.

"I'll ask her if there's any other match for Thảo," Thân explained.

Mrs. Thân smiled, handing her husband a bowl of instant noodles mixed with seaweed from Korea, before opening the fridge to retrieve a jar of kimchi for the table. Thân liberally drizzled red chili sauce over the noodles, eating and inhaling with determination, as if conveying, "If this strategy fails, I'll come up with another one."

In the evening, after consuming three bowls of rice, Thân placed an international call to Vietnam to speak with his mother. Mrs. Sáu's voice came through the other end of the line,

"Hello!"

"Mom, it's me."

"Oh, it's you."

"How are you, Mom?"

"Have you had breakfast yet?"

"At this hour, I'm already thinking about lunch. Did you just have breakfast?"

"It's almost 10 p.m. here, Mom."

"Late already? Why haven't you put the kids to bed? They need to rest so they can go to school in the morning."

"Both of them are already asleep, Mom. We called to share the good news with 'Grandma'. Nghĩa got the results for his math exam. He scored 95 points, Mom."

"He takes after his father when he was young, excellent at math."

"You know what, Mom? He even said he could easily get 100 points if he rechecked the test before submitting."

"Oh, that boy is too confident. Tell him Grandma doesn't like that kind of carelessness. Next time, remind him to review thoroughly before submitting the test," Mrs. Sáu advised.

"We've told him many times, Mom," Thân responded.

"He's still young; don't scold him too much. It's fortunate that he's doing well in school. Focus on correcting his impulsiveness, not to get overexcited. Help him to change so he has a better chance of success in life later on," Mrs. Sáu advised.

"My, you're truly great, Mom. Every time I talk to you, I'm amazed by your wisdom," Thân remarked.

"What's there to be amazed about? Your father used to teach you guys the same way when he was still alive. I only learned from him. Speaking of which, I just wonder, where did that little one get his overconfidence from?" Mrs. Sáu pondered.

"You're teasing me, Mom. I admire you because what Dad and you taught us align with the latest research findings here," Thân said.

"Our ancestors passed down their teachings, and your father and I tried our best to pass them on to you. We didn't know anything special," Mrs. Sáu humbly responded.

"Mom, you know what? Experts here have confirmed that a person's success in life depends more on their emotional intelligence (EQ) than their intelligence quotient (IQ)," Thân explained.

"What are you talking about?" Mrs. Sáu asked.

"IQ measures intellectual intelligence, while EQ measures a person's emotional intelligence. In essence, studies show that successful people aren't necessarily smarter than others; they are emotionally mature, able to control their own emotions, and sensitive to the emotions of others," Thân elaborated.

"Is that so? Well, we have a saying, 'Anger clouds the mind.' Mature individuals never lose their temper easily," Mrs. Sáu reflected without further explanation.

After discussing their son's matters, Thân shifted to their daughter's issue, attempting to maintain a calm tone. As if he had just remembered, he asked his mother,

"Oh, by the way, what about the matter of finding a husband for our daughter?"

Mrs. Sáu quickly responded, "Good thing you reminded me. Yes, there's a potential match that sounds promising."

Thân chuckled, "This time, to avoid any trouble, make sure to meet all the future in-laws first, Mom."

"I heard he's a single child," Mrs. Sáu added.

"How do you know?" Thân inquired.

"Do you remember our neighbor, Mrs. Năm?" Mrs. Sáu asked.

"Yes, Mom," Thân replied.

"She is the first wife of Mr. Năm, who also has a second wife living in District Two. His second wife has a younger sister who is a close friend of my schoolmate since childhood," Mrs. Sáu explained.

As Mrs. Sáu spoke, Thân anticipated a long 'episode', so he pulled a chair from the dining table and sat down to rest his legs.

After fifteen minutes, Thân learned that through the matchmaking efforts of a friend of a friend highly valued by his mother, she had found a worthy match for their daughter Thảo. The groom-to-be was said to be a Vietnamese-American, about to graduate as a medical doctor. To use the expression 'Once slipping on a melon peel, one would be scared of a coconut peel,' Thân could be said to have slipped on the peel of a Canadian doctor, so when he heard about the American doctor's peel, he shivered! However, in life, when one feels stuck, hope is the key to opening the door to a new future.

Thân excitedly shared the news with his wife, and the couple gathered to look through the three latest family photo albums, searching for a truly beautiful picture of Thảo to send to Vietnam for Mrs. Sáu to proudly show to the family of the groom-to-be.

15. The letter from home

When Mrs. Năm returned from work, as usual, she reached for the front door and instinctively opened the mailbox, retrieving the stack of mail and bringing it inside. Typically, it was filled with flyers and advertisements, occasionally interspersed with bills - electricity, water, gas, credit card statements - the usual headaches of adult life. Yet, she had grown accustomed to this routine.

However, this time felt different. Among the stack of papers in her hand, Mrs. Năm noticed a letter from Vietnam. As always, her heart skipped a beat. Despite recent phone calls with relatives back home, like many Vietnamese expatriates, she treasured each letter from her homeland, every stroke of ink in blue or purple. The pages, reminiscent of student notebooks with faded yellow ruled lines, were delicately handled, examined thoroughly. After reading the letter, she would meticulously reread it, ensuring she hadn't missed any words or meanings.

Amidst the letters, there lay a photograph. Mrs. Năm's eyes widened in surprise as she brought the photo closer for inspection. She couldn't fathom why Đức's grandmother from Vietnam had sent it. Hastily, she read the accompanying letter and couldn't suppress a laugh. How ironic! Đức's grandmother sought to introduce a bride to her grandson, having spent a whole year searching, only to find Thảo. It was undoubtedly a photo from the Thai hotpot party two months prior, Mrs. Năm was certain.

The weight Mrs. Năm had carried in her heart for the past three months suddenly lifted with each line of her mother-in-law's letter, which she had pored over repeatedly. Seated on the sofa, gazing out the window, she eagerly awaited Đức's return to share the good news. The mere thought of the excitement in her son's eyes, the joy in his smile, suffused her heart with harmonious happiness.

Mrs. Năm observed her son's excitement and, upon his request for permission, promptly ran upstairs to make a phone call informing Thảo. She reminded her son, "Let the elders talk first," and added, "Marriage is a serious matter, experienced only once in a lifetime. Allow me to initiate the conversation with her parents. In fact, I was contemplating inviting your grandmother to represent our family. It's not only to honor her but also to pay tribute to your father's memory."

Inside, "Doctor" Đức felt elated, and even if Mrs. Năm had imposed conditions like leaping into a hot frying pan or traversing a sea of fire, he would obediently adhere to his mother's wishes.

After dinner, the mother and son sat in front of the TV to watch Vietnamese music videos. However, the atmosphere didn't lend itself to enjoying the music. Mrs. Năm lovingly looked at her son and asked, "Seriously, if it were a picture of another girl, what would you say? Will you listen to me?"

Đức didn't hesitate to reply, "You know I will never make you sad."

Mrs. Năm pressed for a more direct answer from Đức. "Would you agree to marry another girl?"

Đức tried to stall for time, saying, "Mom, you know we have the saying, 'The father's merit is like Mount Thái Sơn; The mother's grace is like water flowing from its source.'"

Mrs. Năm interrupted firmly, "I keep reminding you, I gave birth to you, son. So don't think you can evade my questions with answers open to interpretation like that."

"What I mean is, with all the sacrifices you've made for me, of course, I have to appreciate and live in a way that is worthy of your love."

"You still haven't answered my question, dear."

"I think if I were to go to school and earn a degree just to marry a wealthy girl or something like that, then truly, I wouldn't be deserving of your sacrifices at all," Đức pondered for a moment and continued.

"Thank you, mom, for raising me to be a kind person and giving me a compassionate heart, so I can lead a more meaningful life by sharing love with others, whether in relationships or in my profession, where I can alleviate the pain of others. But I know I'm just a small grain of sand. I can only hope that in every decision I make in life, I won't do anything to bring shame to your sacrifices."

Mrs. Năm felt relieved and hugged her son tightly, tears streaming down her face. She wished Thảo were there beside them so she could embrace her and apologize.

On the other house, Mrs. Thân stood in the kitchen, kneading dough for making cakes. After finishing his coffee, Thân took the spoon and headed to the sink behind his wife to wash it. Mrs. Thân, as if she had eyes behind her, teased, "Washing just a spoon, and you wasted so much water."

"You're too conservative. Water doesn't cost much. When I first came here to mow lawns for people, I saw everyone pouring water freely, watering their lawns all day. Sometimes they forget, and water sprays all night."

"Excuse me, are you talking about the old days? Now, to protect the environment, water and electricity companies are urging people to use them judiciously to avoid wasting energy."

"Electricity I can understand, but water, what does it have to do with energy? Besides, do we lack water in Canada? Every spring, when the snow melts, it floods the rivers."

"Look who's talking. The other day, our daughter explained it, and you didn't bother to listen. She said at school, the teacher taught that clean water coming to our house has to pass through a water treatment plant. That plant requires a considerable amount of energy to operate water pumps. Moreover, wastewater needs to be treated. The more wastewater, the more energy needed for treatment. And any energy source affects the living environment to some extent."

Thân grinned and chuckled, "Actually, I've heard someone predict that after religious wars, the world will witness wars over drinking water."

"Why is that?"

"Because water sources in many places around the world, including in the U.S., are starting to decline or run dry."

As Thân spoke, he entered the computer room to prepare income tax documents for the Nails salons.

The phone on the kitchen shelf suddenly rang. "Who's calling at this hour?" Mrs. Thân grumbled but still hastily washed her dough-covered hands to answer the phone. On the other end of the line, Mrs. Năm recounted everything for Mrs. Thân. If Mrs. Năm was astonished after reading the letter from Đức's grandmother this afternoon, Mrs. Thân was ten times more surprised listening to Mrs. Năm retell the story.

The two 'sisters', each holding one end of the phone, burst into laughter with tears streaming down their faces. After regaining their composure, Mrs. Thân expressed her curiosity, "Do you know, 'sister' Năm, a few months ago Thảo's grandmother asked us to choose a picture of Thảo to send to her. But I heard that it was for some family of a doctor in the U.S. to look at. Who would have thought?"

Mrs. Năm pondered for a moment, "Maybe it's because when I was at the refugee camp initially, I thought I would go to the U.S., so I asked the Red Cross to send messages to the family like that. Until now, I realize there are still misunderstandings among some relatives."

The two 'sisters', or more accurately, the two partners in-laws now, quickly set aside that matter and agreed to continue discussing their children's future at the shop the next day. Dropping the phone, Mrs. Thân called out to her husband as if enemies were approaching, as the Vietnamese saying goes. She urged Thân, "Sit down here and listen." Mrs. Thân began to recount the entire story from start to finish.

Thân, of course, was equally surprised. Now feeling the need to pull up a chair, he muttered, "Strange, indeed." He suddenly recalled the widely circulated words of the U.S. Secretary of Defense from some time ago and concluded, "People say it right: In life, you can plan and prepare for what you know you know, and even for what you know you don't know. But for what you don't know you don't know, that's a whole different story."

So the two families went with the flow, pushing the boat along. They planned the engagement first, waiting until Thảo finished university for the wedding.

During her university days, on lucky days, Thảo would be fortunate enough to have Doctor Đức pick her up in his car to go for lunch. After their engagement day, Đức treated himself to a yellow Volkswagen Beetle, the classic model, but for the two lovers, it was their first 'Yellow Frog' together. The two often visit the park in front of the Manitoba legislative building to relive their parents' past. Sitting on the green grass, under the warm sunlight, they contemplate the statue of the Golden Boy, sharing plump red cherries with each other.

From then on, Thảo was often seen visiting the pediatric hospital, where doctor Đức worked, to see the young patients. Each time she went, she never forgot to bring a bottle of pink nail polish for children, to beautify and bring joy to them. When you think about it, isn't that a noble contribution from the nail industry? Bringing joy to life.

- The End -

Notes

1. Poem: 'Đoạn Trường Tân Thanh' (The Tale of Kiều); Author: Nguyễn Du.
2. Song: 'Kỷ Vật Cho Em'; Songwriter: Phạm Duy.
3. Play: 'Người Vợ Không Bao Giờ Cưới'; Playwright: Kiên Giang.
4. Play: 'Tình Anh Bán Chiếu'; Playwright: Viễn Châu.
5. Song: 'Trường Ca Con Đường Cái Quan'; Songwriter: Phạm Duy.
6. Song: 'Một Chuyến Bay Đêm'; Songwriters: Song Ngọc & Hoài Linh.

Author

Vinh Quyen Tang
(Tăng Quyền Vinh)
Ottawa, Canada.

Books published:
1. Bên Kia Bến Đỗ, 2021
    Tứ Quý (Truyện trích từ Bên Kia Bến Đỗ), 2024.
2. Đứa Con An Giang, 2022
3. Lu nước ngọt, 2023
4. Nails Tình Thương, 2023
5. The Boy From An Giang: A Journey Through AI-Assisted Translation, 2023 (Under revision)
6. The Precious Quartet (Selected Tales from Bên Kia Bến Đỗ), 2024
7. Compassionate Nails: A Journey of Love and Resilience (Translated from the Vietnamese title 'Nails Tình Thương'), 2024

ISBN 978-1-7381921-4-4